HAA...

BOLD IN WAR AND LOVE

The Viking chief who had threatened Wulf was now staring at Rosamund in a way that would have made her blush under other circumstances. Her heart pounded in her throat, and she felt an inexplicable force within her, drawing her toward him. There was something in his voice, perhaps, or his eyes. Or perhaps she was being drawn to her death.

"You are the leader of these men, Haakon Olesson." She swallowed, then her face was a mask again. "I desire to speak with you privately."

Haakon smiled, and they moved to a corner of the great hall, where she turned to face the huge Viking.

"You have won only part of your victory tonight, Haakon Olesson. I will pledge no interference from my people in your removal of booty. But you must swear not to burn or rape or destroy the hold. You must pledge that your men will have only those women who consent."

"I will swear," Haakon said. "Now, will you agree to be taken? I desire you."

Rosamund felt a shock course through her system and she nearly lost her balance. "Haakon Olesson, you may have me, by my own consent."

THE GOLDEN AX

Eric Neilson

Created by the producers of
Wagons West, White Indian,
Saga of the Southwest, and
The Kent Family Chronicles Series.

Chairman of the Board: Lyle Kenyon Engel

BANTAM BOOKS
TORONTO · NEW YORK · LONDON · SYDNEY

HAAKON 1: THE GOLDEN AX
*A Bantam Book / published by arrangement with
Book Creations, Inc.*

Bantam edition / March 1984

*Produced by Book Creations, Inc.
Chairman of the Board: Lyle Kenyon Engel.*

ISBN 0-553-23639-3

Published simultaneously in the United States and Canada

---

*Bantam Books are published by Bantam Books, Inc. Its trade-
mark, consisting of the words "Bantam Books" and the por-
trayal of a rooster, is Registered in U.S. Patent and Trademark
Office and in other countries. Marca Registrada. Bantam
Books, Inc., 666 Fifth Avenue, New York, New York 10103.*

PRINTED IN THE UNITED STATES OF AMERICA

H   0 9 8 7 6 5 4 3 2 1

Prologue

They were called Vikings.

From the end of the eighth century through the eleventh, they sailed out from Norway, Denmark, and Sweden in graceful longships. They sailed as far west as Greenland and Newfoundland, and in the east they reached Constantinople.

Sometimes they raided, and at other times in other places they conquered and settled. They ruled in the Shetlands, the Orkneys, and the Western Isles of Scotland. They founded cities along the western coast of Ireland. They ruled in the north and east of England; for part of the eleventh century, under the Dane Knut the Great, they ruled the whole country. The king of France made a Viking chief the duke of Normandy. The emperors of Constantinople recruited their elite troops, the Varangian Guards, from these men of the North. The Vikings sailed along the great rivers of Russia in search of trade and founded towns, which grew into Russian kingdoms.

Raiders and pirates, ironhanded conquerors and rulers, they also worked in wood, iron, and silver, built ships as strong and seaworthy as they were beautiful, brewed ale and mead, caught fish, built houses, and left a legacy that has not been forgotten in a thousand years.

They recorded their deeds on rune-stones raised above the graves of their dead or in verses and stories that still ring like a battle-ax on a shield. These were the Norsemen—"Men of the North." We call them Vikings.

THE GOLDEN AX

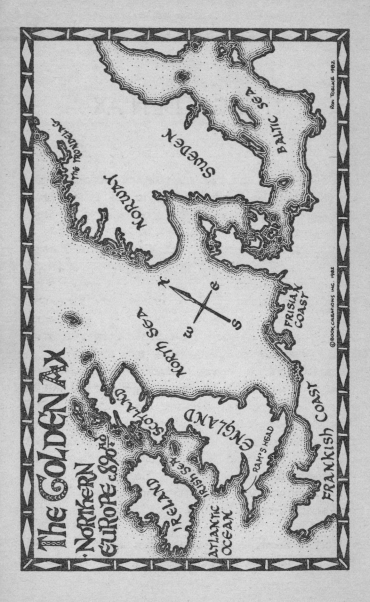

The Golden Ax

Northern Europe 890 A.D.

THE TRONDELAG

NORWAY

SWEDEN

BALTIC SEA

Ron Toelke 1982

© Book Creations Inc. 1982

NORTH SEA

SCOTLAND

ENGLAND

IRELAND

IRISH SEA

RAM'S HEAD

ATLANTIC OCEAN

FRISIAN COAST

FRANKISH COAST

N
E
S
W

1

By Christian reckoning it was the year 893.

A century ago the first ships of the Norsemen had glided out of the North Sea fogs to fall on the great monastery of Lindisfarne off the north coast of England. The Norsemen had slain the monks, looted the monastery's treasures, and sent terror echoing throughout Europe.

On nearly every coast from Scotland to Egypt, the people kept a fearful watch for the approach of lean dragon ships. Many Viking chieftains and warriors returned home with gold and silver, weapons and slaves. A few came home battered and without booty. Some did not come home at all. Reefs and storms and enemy swords took their toll.

A leader unlucky in raiding and battle could turn to trade so his men might not return empty-handed and his ship not lie neglected on the shore. A wise chief knew that it was both honorable and prudent to provide for the men who had sworn to follow and obey him, whether they profited by the sword or by trading. Ships that carried warriors to the shores of France, England, and Ireland also carried wool and slaves and soapstone vessels to the markets of Birka and Hedeby.

West of Scotland the sea stretches gray and endless toward the horizon. In early autumn, storms can sweep in from the western sea to sink the strongest ship or smash her against the fanged rocks of the islands and the coast of the mainland. So Bjorn Karlsson, helmsman of the long-ship *Red Hawk*, kept a careful eye on the horizon. He'd sailed in swift longships and broad-beamed *knarrs* for twenty-five of his forty years, and there was little he did not know about the sea and the weather between Iceland and the coast of Finland. Today at least would end as fair as it had started, although the breeze from the west was brisk and the waves were growing white manes of foam. Even as heavily loaded as she was, *Red Hawk* rode grace-fully over the waves. The square sail with its red and green stripes billowed out from the mast amidships, round-ed and firm like a woman's breast. Bjorn sighed at that last thought. This past summer they'd had no luck in finding women—or anything else, for that matter.

They'd set out at the beginning of the sailing season, thirty-eight good men ready to follow Haakon Olesson wherever he might lead them. Haakon—called "The Dark" for his hair and beard—was still short of thirty, but he'd fought so well in Odo's great invasion of France three years before, he had had little difficulty filling his ship with men who trusted him.

But they soon found that other Norsemen had stripped the Frankish coasts of nearly all loot except weapons and armor, and of all women under sixty or over twelve. Foul weather kept the *Red Hawk* away from those parts of England where it was possible to raid, then storms drove them onto the coast of Wales. They lost five weary weeks there repairing the ship. The coast of Moslem Spain offered rich booty, but it was too strongly guarded to be safely raided by a single ship, no matter how well manned.

There were women in Ireland, but also in Ireland were Haakon's enemies. Olaf Haraldsson, who had stolen the lands of Haakon's father and driven him back to Norway in defeat and shame, had sons and sworn friends there, all of them with fighting men and ships. Irish waters were not safe for Haakon Olesson and only a single ship.

At last Haakon had taken *Red Hawk* north to Iceland. Hope of good raiding was ending along with the summer. Bringing home a cargo was the next best course, and in the far north, Iceland was the best place for trading.

There were five thousand Norsemen in Iceland, and thousands of sheep, goats, and tough little ponies. A ship could find a good cargo there — the heavy, warm cloth called wadmal, sheepskins, ropes made of walrus hide, whale ivory, furs, kegs of salt. Haakon was as shrewd at trading as he was cunning and valiant in battle, and waged a good price for the swords, helmets, and bars of iron gathered up along the Frankish coast. Landed at Hedeby or Birka, *Red Hawk's* cargo would put a good handful of silver in each man's pouch, and hopefully no one would call this summer's voyage a failure, or Haakon a bad leader.

Bjorn Karlsson sighed. A rumbling in his belly reminded him that dinnertime was approaching. He looked forward, where Haakon stood in the bow of the ship, his sword hand gripping the upswept prow, holding him upright. Haakon looked broader than usual in his heavy, blue wadmal cloak, and darker than ever with his skin burned by a summer at sea in the sun and wind. The breeze ruffled his square-cut brown beard. Standing still, Haakon could sometimes be taken for a farmer or even a thrall, but when he picked up sword and shield and put his heavy-framed body into motion, no one could doubt for a moment that he was a warrior.

Suddenly Haakon stiffened and raised one hand, shading his eyes as he looked into the westering sun. Bjorn turned in the same direction and searched the sea. His other hand clamped down tightly on the long bar of the steering oar.

There! Dark against the pale blue sky, the sail of another longship was lifting over the horizon.

In the bow of *Red Hawk*, Haakon Olesson stood watching the other ship move closer. She was a dragon ship, considerably larger than *Red Hawk*. Her sail was a patched and faded pattern of black and yellow squares. On her present course she would come up with *Red Hawk* as both ships passed into the lee of a small, rocky island off to starboard. The water there would be calm, good for fighting from ship to ship.

Haakon studied the other ship again. One that size could carry at least sixty men and possibly as many as eighty. An attack by *Red Hawk* would face heavy odds and would make no sense in any case. Haakon decided he would give the chief of the approaching ship no reason to fight as long as the man gave him none.

He would also not sit with his hands folded while the other ship came up. In these lonely waters were lawless men and also men who might be made lawless by temptation and the hope of their crimes going undetected. Haakon would raise the shield of peace on his mast, but would be ready with his war shield on his left arm.

Haakon let go of the prow and took a deep breath, then

cupped both hands around his mouth. His shout easily carried the length of *Red Hawk*.

"*Hooooo-a!* Longship coming! We raise the peace shield, but we arm ourselves! Make ready!"

Haakon's men opened the ironbound wooden chests, which served as seats for rowing, and began pulling out weapons and armor. Each man always kept at hand a spear, an ax, or a sword, wrapped in sealskin against the salt air and spray. The rest of their war gear lay in these chests. Their raiding in France had left them well equipped. Men who had set sail in linen shirts now wore stout jackets of boiled leather, and men who had been bareheaded in the spring now had helmets. Men who had wielded old swords handed down from great-grandsires now had sharp blades of the best Frankish steel. A dozen men now had knee-length mail shirts, Haakon and Bjorn among them. If it came to a fight, Haakon knew his men could give a good account of themselves against any odds the approaching ship could offer.

Bjorn was the last man to arm himself. Haakon came aft to take the steering oar while the helmsman pulled on his armor, then picked up shield and sword. By the time Bjorn was armed, the other ship was almost within bow-shot. Haakon and Bjorn stood side by side, watching her intently.

More than just the patched and faded sail told that the other ship had taken hard knocks. Large areas of her sides were bare of paint, and both bow and stern were gouged and battered. Her mast showed a grayish-white streak where a split was roughly bolstered with a heavy piece of driftwood.

Amidships, the other crew was gathering and arming. A

quick count of heads told Haakon there were about fifty of them, fewer than he'd expected. None seemed to have more armor than a helmet and a quilted or leather shirt. All carried weapons and well-scarred shields. They looked lean, hungry, and fierce, like a pack of wolves after a long and bitter winter.

The other ship's helmsman stared at the *Red Hawk* for a moment. Then he shouted an order. Two of his men bent down and raised a triangular shield to a hook on the mast, point upward.

"They're also raising the peace shield," said Bjorn. "That's good. I can't see what a fight with them would give except blood. I suspect their luck's been even worse than ours."

"Perhaps," said Haakon in a cool voice. Their luck on this summer's voyage wasn't his favorite topic of conversation. Besides, he wondered what a peace shield, hoisted by such a wild-looking crew, meant. Certainly Bjorn was right about the wastefulness of fighting such men when there was another choice.

The other longship rode higher than the *Red Hawk* with her heavy cargo. Slowly she drew ahead until her steering oar was level with *Red Hawk*'s bow. It looked as if the other crew also saw that nothing would be gained by a fight except bloodshed and needless widows and orphans.

Suddenly there was rattling and clattering, thudding feet and a swirl of movement aboard the other ship as her men sprang to their oars. The ship began to swing as the oars on the far side dug into the water and the helmsman heaved on the steering oar. The ship sliced across *Red Hawk*'s prow, rising high above her. Wood squealed, groaned, and cracked as *Red Hawk* drove forward against the vessel.

Red Hawk quivered from stem to stern, half of Haakon's men reeled and staggered from the jolt, and some of them fell to the deck. Haakon bellowed a curse on that dragon ship and everyone in her, then leaped down onto *Red Hawk's* main deck.

He'd barely landed when the other ship's helmsman, a swarthy rogue in leather breeches, sprang up onto the railing, waving his sword and now carrying a shield as well. "At them, at them, at them!" the helmsman roared. "Slay, slay, give us the day!"

One of his men threw a loop of rope over the dragon's head on *Red Hawk's* prow, binding the two vessels together. Others leaped down onto Haakon's deck, howling like the wolves they resembled. A spear whistled through the air from the enemy ship, and one of Haakon's men shouted as it tore through his leather shirt into his shoulder.

Haakon was furious. Even though he'd been suspicious about the other ship's hungry crew, he hadn't really expected anyone would be mad enough to attack. It was double treachery to battle under the peace shield, hideous to both men and gods. If word of it ever reached other Norsemen . . .

But why should word of this treachery not be swallowed up in the sea, silently and completely? The island to windward was a featureless, barren wall of gray rock, and there were no other ships in sight. If none appeared in the next hour, the enemy's villainy could go forever undetected. If they won, they would not leave even one of Haakon's men alive to tell what had happened. If they saw they were losing, they would fight desperately, knowing they were doomed with no hope of mercy from the victors.

Haakon's thoughts leaped forward to grasp the situation.

For both crews, this battle was win or die. He raised his shield and drew his sword.

"Bjorn, stay at the helm. It's my order."

"But—"

"I said it was my order." He slapped the older man on his mail-covered shoulder. "Come, my friend, do you think this is the last battle we'll see together?"

Bjorn laughed. "Hardly."

"Good." Haakon filled his massive chest, then roared: "Stand, stand, men of *Red Hawk*! Make these swine pay for their treachery! Our luck is turning! The gods have sent these wretches to us for a sacrifice!" Then he barged forward, clearing a path through his own men with his shield and the flat of his sword.

As he ran, he saw his men form a defensive line across *Red Hawk*'s deck, a line as stiff as a drawn bowstring, but the enemy was still leaping aboard. Steel rang and shields collided. In places, Haakon's men were outnumbered two to one. Plank by plank they were giving up *Red Hawk*'s deck.

Then Haakon reached their line. At fifteen he'd beaten grown men in wrestling. At twenty he could carry a ram under each arm, or a soapstone washing trough on one shoulder. He plunged into the battle so fast that neither he nor his first opponent had time to swing swords. Haakon stiffened his arm, and his shield smashed the other's sword arm back across his chest. The man went over backward, his shield swinging wide as he fell. Before he struck the deck Haakon's sword whistled down with the speed of Thor's hammer and split the man from chin to stomach. Haakon leaped over him to a new enemy.

A spear drove down toward Haakon. His shield rose to

meet it. The spearhead pierced the leather-covered wood, nearly skewering Haakon as it flashed by his ear. He swung the shield, and the shaft of the embedded spear lashed through the ranks of the enemy. A man screamed and clapped his hand to his face, where jaw and cheek and one eye were bloody wreckage. One of Haakon's men closed in and struck with an ax. The man's screams died as his head lolled on his shoulders. The thud of the falling body was lost in the swelling uproar of clashing weapons and cries of panting men.

Haakon saw that he'd made the enemy pause. He stepped back a few feet, jerked the rest of the spear from the shield, and hurled it at the enemy. Around him the battle cries of his own men were beginning to rise.

"Haakon!"

"*Red Hawk!*"

The enemy was still screaming "Slay! Slay!" and howling with a terrible hatred and fury. Haakon doubted that the cries of Ragnarok itself would be more dreadful—should his fate lead him to Valhalla and a chance to stand beside the gods in that last great battle against evil.

Through all the uproar and confusion, Haakon could see that the enemy was no longer gaining control of *Red Hawk's* deck. His men were holding them just forward of the mast. The battle raged over and around the bales and barrels of cargo. Men tumbled over bundles of walrus tusks and fell down to be speared or slashed as they struggled to recover their footing. They poured out their lifeblood over bales of wadmal cloth.

Now Haakon's men edged forward, his bellowed orders gathering them together until their shields formed a solid wall. Their better armor repelled weapons swung or hurled against them, while their own swords and axes bit through flimsy linen and leather into flesh. Behind Haakon's line his best archer, Hagar the Simple, strung his bow and began shooting at men on the enemy's deck. Perhaps Hagar was short on wits and words, but he was the best archer Haakon had ever seen.

The enemy's leader was perched on his ship's railing, waving his sword and urging his men on. Both Thorkell and Hagar sent three arrows at him, but each time, the man leaped safely down out of sight. Then he jumped up again and went on shouting to his crew.

The man's seeming invulnerability gave Haakon a moment's doubt. Was this a man or some evil spirit risen from Hel to lead the enemy? Then the doubt passed and anger took its place. Neither man nor spirit would stand against him without being challenged!

Haakon's eyes fell on the oars lashed along either side of *Red Hawk*. He knelt and pulled one out of its lashings. It was as long as three tall men, but Haakon lifted it with ease. Then he grasped the shaft with both hands and swung the blade at the enemy leader. The oar blade caught the man across both knees and he sent out a scream that showed he was no spirit. Then he sat hard on empty air and vanished behind the railing of his ship with a crash and another scream.

Their leader's fall made the enemy pause and give up more of *Red Hawk*'s deck. Haakon saw this and charged. By sheer weight and speed he crashed through the enemy's line. His impact knocked two men from his path and hurled one of them to the deck. Haakon kicked the fallen one in the ribs, then turned as the other thrust at him with a spear. He hacked at the spear as his mail caught and held the point. The shaft splintered. Haakon's sword swung downward and struck the spearman in the leg. On his good leg the man hopped out of Haakon's reach. Haakon let him go, for his attention was now on the enemy's deck.

He charged again, reaching *Red Hawk*'s bow. He sprang up on the railing and balanced there. His sword whistled, carving a steel circle around him, driving the enemy defenders back from their ship's railing. When he looked back, he saw that the enemy's line had closed behind him across *Red Hawk*'s deck. He was alone, but the way ahead lay clear, and he'd come too far to retreat now. Haakon leaped.

The men on the other ship's deck flinched as Haakon's two hundred pounds hurled at them. The toe of one boot caught on the railing. For a heart-stopping moment he expected to fall back into the sea or crash down helplessly on the deck. He landed, staggering, but on his feet. Again he swept his sword in a wide arc to clear his flanks, then gave a shout and closed with an enemy.

The man stood his ground but carelessly held his shield too far from his body. Haakon hooked the rim of his own shield behind the other's and jerked. The opponent's shield swung aside, and Haakon's sword carved its way through the gap. One cut smashed the man's shoulder and the second took him in the side of the neck. The dying man lurched forward, so that Haakon had to thrust the falling body aside before he could turn to meet the next attack.

Now three men together came at Haakon. None of them was a particularly good fighter, but they came on with the desperate, mindless courage that can make for a deadly opponent.

Fortunately, Haakon had room to shift position. Without it he might have died under their rush. By now two thirds or more of the enemy's fighters were on *Red Hawk's* deck, dead, dying, or on the defense. Aboard their own ship, the enemy was scattered and thin.

Haakon retreated, shifting to the right as he did and moving as quickly as he did when he attacked. Then he suddenly darted forward, around the flank of the oncoming men. As the closest one turned to face him, Haakon struck ferociously. The man's shield leaped up into position, but Haakon's sword split the shield as if it had been made of parchment. Haakon slashed again. This time the sword cut through leather and wool into the man's thigh. Then Haakon's enemies were backing away from him. In another moment he saw why.

Thorkell, waving an ax, stood on the deck behind Haakon. He was a tall, broad man in his first season with Haakon, a welcome addition to the band. Thorkell was an enthusiastic fighter, who grunted and cursed throughout the battle, but with a wide, flyaway grin on his face from the first blow to the last. Behind him three more of *Red Hawk's* men were climbing over the railing. Thorkell gave a wild cry and rushed forward. The men who'd backed away from Haakon turned and ran. Perhaps they thought Haakon and Thorkell were berserkers—those warrior-madmen were the most fearful human enemy a man could face, and it was no shame to flee from them.

Haakon waved his sword over his head. His three men leaped down from the railing, followed Thorkell, and caught the fleeing men as they retreated toward the bow.

Haakon was about to join them when Black Ayolf called him a warning as a new opponent seemed to rise out of the deck at his feet. He was a burly, black-haired man who carried an ironbound club and a shield the size of a small tabletop. The club crashed down on Haakon's shield. The shield did not split, but for a moment Haakon thought his left arm might. His sword carved bits out of the other's shield, spraying sparks and splinters of wood. The black-haired man had almost Haakon's own strength and absorbed the pounding. Gradually he edged Haakon away from the other fighters, raining blows on his shield. Haakon began to wonder how long his shield would stay in one piece, how long even his good Frankish sword would keep its edge.

Back and forth across the ship's deck, the two men went swinging and slashing at each other. At one moment Haakon had the better and was driving the black-haired warrior backward. In the next moment it was the black-haired man who was attacking and Haakon who was backing away, watching for pools of blood and sprawled bodies. He and the black-haired man were so evenly matched, it would be a quick end for whoever first lost his balance.

Sweat ran down Haakon's face. His head began to ache from the continuous crashing of club and sword on shield. His breath bubbled hot in his throat. He knew that the sounds of battle around him were dying away. Several men were shouting for mercy. He assumed they were the enemy. Vaguely, he had the strange feeling that someone was reciting poetry. This was hard to believe, though not impossible. Perhaps the Valkyries of Odin were hovering close, ready to lift up Haakon's dead and bear them to Valhalla.

He could see that his opponent was gradually wearing down. The club crashed against Haakon's shield less often and less hard. He found it easy to block the blows. The sheer size of the man's shield kept Haakon from dealing a killing stroke, but he managed to draw blood three times, in the arm, in the leg, and from the temple just below the man's mane of black hair. Haakon had the advantage now, and he pressed harder. The black-haired man was desperate. Desperate men could be as deadly in battle as berserkers.

The club crashed down on Haakon's shield with all its original strength and speed. Haakon saw the man draw his weapon back slowly, as if it suddenly weighed as much as a ship's anchor stone. Haakon shifted his footing cautiously, holding back his reply. The club swung again, and Haakon crouched to get in under the blow, catching the club on the upper rim of his shield. The metal of the rim buckled, the wood splintered and cracked. The iron head of the club whistled past Haakon's head, and he twisted so that it missed crushing his shoulder. Then he swung his sword at the man's arm before it could be pulled back. The sword slashed the black-haired man's arm open to the bone, but he made no sound. He stepped back, let his club drop, then stood in exhausted silence, his disabled arm hanging at his side, blood dripping from his fingers onto the deck.

Haakon realized that the next gesture was up to him. It took an immense effort of will to rearrange his mind so that he could speak sensible words.

"Do you yield?"

The black-haired man looked surprised. "I can?"

That was a reasonable question. The man had played his part in an act of foul, godless treachery. He was probably expecting Haakon to cut him down where he stood.

Haakon found his thoughts flowing freely once more. He nodded. "Throw down your shield and kneel."

The man obeyed. Haakon stepped back and looked around. Slowly, he sorted what he saw into distinct pictures.

The blood-streaked decks of both ships were littered with sprawled or crumpled bodies and discarded weapons and armor. Most of the bodies were those of the attackers, and most of the men still on their feet were Haakon's. Some showed open wounds and staggered as they tried to stand, but a good two thirds of *Red Hawk*'s men seemed to be still alive and more or less whole.

On the other hand, the attackers had met the bad luck they deserved. No more than twenty-five of them were still able to kneel or crouch at the feet of Haakon's men. Doubtless the enemy began crying for mercy when they saw the battle going against them. Haakon was glad his men had listened to those cries. Even if the enemy deserved death, he did not savor killing men as they cried for mercy.

Forward on the deck of the enemy's ship stood Bjorn and a bony-faced man, a head taller than Haakon but as slender as a spear, clean-shaven, and fair. He held a sword in one hand and a shield on the other arm. His blue eyes met Haakon's. Then as if the meeting of eyes were a command, he spoke a short passage of verse:

"Crews clashed on the waves commingling.
Edge met edge, and ash shields splintered.

But the guileful Leatherbreeches got little good
From the fight he forced, for his foe,
Great of heart, won all in the end."

Haakon looked at Bjorn. Bjorn returned the glance, but
less comfortably, knowing he had disobeyed orders by
taking part in the battle.

"I told you to stay at the helm," said Haakon to his
comrade.

"It seemed to me," Bjorn replied, "that we needed steel
on the enemy's deck rather than a hand at *Red Hawk*'s
helm."

Haakon laughed. "Well, perhaps we did. But we also
need men who know and obey an order when they hear
one."

Bjorn nodded proudly, and Haakon knew the matter
could be left there. Bjorn always found it hard to stay out
of a good fight, and he was not a man to be hammered into
obedience. If he'd been like that, Haakon wouldn't have
put him at the helm of *Red Hawk*. Yet Bjorn also knew
exactly what might weaken Haakon's leadership and always stopped short of that point.

Haakon stepped forward and faced the poet. "Do you
yield?"

"Will you admit that I did not dishonor myself by taking
part in the treachery against you?"

"I'll admit nothing I haven't seen with my own eyes or
done with my own hands," replied Haakon. He looked
around. "Can anyone here say if he's telling the truth?"

"I think he is," said Bjorn. "I certainly didn't see him on
Red Hawk's deck all during the battle. I didn't see him
strike a blow after we boarded this ship, either."

Several more of Haakon's men nodded at Bjorn's words.

"That's what I say, too," Thorkell spoke up.

"Aye, indeed. He didn't do anything in the fight but stand up there," Black Ayolf verified.

"No, jarl, not quite," said one. "He started making verses when we got close enough to hear him. I thought he was mad. But he never lifted that ax against us, not that I saw."

Haakon held up a hand for silence. "It seems you have witnesses enough on your side from among my own men. You may yield, and I will admit you did nothing treacherous today."

The blond man bowed his head. "I, Gunnar Thorsten, thank you:

> An ax lord shall always honor skalds
> With worthy gifts of spun gold—
> His name shall be known abroad in life,
> And when death falls, be long remembered."

Haakon smiled. He was glad he wouldn't have to make an enemy of a poet or be known as the man who'd put one to death. A warrior's reputation was in the hands of poets when his sword could no longer win battles.

"I thank you for the praise. For the moment there's nothing I can offer you but your life and honor in return for your verses. Will that be enough?"

"It will be." Gunnar put down his shield and ax and sat down on the deck. Haakon turned and hurried aft, looking for the enemy leader.

He found that the man wearing the leather breeches had somehow made his way into the low shelter under the aft deck. Apparently dead, he was lying on his back. Four bedraggled slave women cowered in the corners, avoiding their former master as if he were diseased or cursed. Well, perhaps any man who would launch such a dishonorable attack could rightly be called both.

At least the man died with the courage of despair. Even if Haakon had shown him mercy, the man would still be crippled for life. Suddenly, the prostrate form moved swiftly and drew a knife from his belt, striking at Haakon.

The point of the knife caught in Haakon's mail and did not penetrate flesh. Haakon's massive right hand snatched the man's wrist. He twisted viciously until the man grunted in pain and the knife clattered to the deck. Then Haakon's sword rose as high as the low overhead would permit. It was not a heavy blow, but the diabolical leader never moved again.

Haakon backed out onto the deck, holding his battered and bloody sword. He stood up, wiped the sweat out of his eyes with the back of his hand, and surveyed the scene of his victory.

II

When they saw him, Haakon's men cheered wildly and beat their spears and swords against their shields. It sounded like the weapons-taking ceremony when all the men of the area acclaim a new war leader. To Haakon the noise seemed almost as loud as the battle itself, and it made his weary head throb.

"Enough!" he shouted. "Today *we* have the victory!

Today *our* luck has turned! Let us see what we've won before it grows dark." The sun was halfway down toward the western horizon, and there was a great deal of work to be done before nightfall. Haakon remembered the words of Odo the Dane when the Norse host was withdrawing from Paris:

"The chieftain's work doesn't stop with the end of the fighting. He shouldn't sleep easily until the last of his men is buried or safe at home with ale in his stomach and a woman in his arms. Odin asks this of any Viking at the head of fighting men." Odo himself had the responsibility for over seven thousand men. Haakon hoped he could do as well with his little shipload.

A quick count by Bjorn told Haakon that his losses were mercifully small. Four men were dead, and two more had wounds that would almost certainly kill them. Five others were hurt badly enough so they would not be pulling an oar or lifting a sword for a while.

"Our fortunes may finally have turned indeed," said Haakon. "I wouldn't have dared even to pray for losses so light."

"I think our luck really turned a while back on the Frankish coast," said Bjorn. "We grumbled at the time, but it was the armor and those good Frankish swords that brought us through this fight."

A quick inspection made it clear there wouldn't be much booty from the captured ship. There was nothing except the bodies and weapons of her crew, the four terrified women, and the most miserable food and ship's gear. The ship herself—the prisoners called her *Wave Walker*—was another matter. Haakon was no master shipwright, but he'd sailed in almost every type of craft from the curraghs of Ireland to the pleasure boats of great jarls. Like any wise Norse chief, he knew a good deal about ships, which could either be his death or his fortune, and what Haakon didn't know, Bjorn did.

The two men studied *Wave Walker* from bow to stern. At last they stood up, brushed the bilge slime from their clothes, and looked at each other. Haakon was the first to speak what was in both their minds.

"The ship herself is the best piece of booty we've found."

"I agree. She's been badly used, but she was built well by men who wanted their work to last."

"They succeeded. A winter's work, not sparing the silver, and she'll be fit to carry a king into battle."

"Indeed. She makes me think of a fine hunting dog kept chained and starved. We have to free her from her bad masters and fatten her up."

Haakon laughed. "We shall, though she's certainly not going to be an easy piece of booty to take home. We have enough *Red Hawk* men to guard our prisoners and sail our own ship, but hardly more than—" He broke off, his mind pursuing a new and extraordinary line of thought. One hand came up and gripped his beard as he seemed almost withdrawn from reality.

Bjorn was silent. He knew what lay behind that expression. Haakon was thinking, and he would soon come up with some cunning scheme.

Haakon's hand finally unclenched. "We'd have less trouble with our prisoners if we could get them to join us. Then we'd have enough—"

Bjorn stared at his young leader in astonishment. "Take men who've outlawed themselves by their treachery, if they weren't outlawed before? What's rotted your wits that you—"

"I think my wits are sound. Consider how it is: These men are outlaws, as you said. They have yielded to us, but by law and custom they still can't be sure of anything except death or slavery. Sooner or later they'll realize this and then they'll be desperate. Who knows what they might do, or how many of us might die? Even if there's no more blood, we'd still lose sleep and strength guarding them.

"But if we let them swear loyalty to me and comradeship with all of us, they'll no longer be outlaws desperate with fear. They should be willing at least to help us take *Wave Walker* home. That itself is no small service, and who knows? If they sail with us as free men with a chance to regain their honor, they may even be willing to stand by us in a fight. We still have a long road home, and any long road has wolves and bandits."

Bjorn nodded slowly. "You make more sense than I first thought. But what if we're lucky again and make a successful raid? The more men to share the loot, the smaller each man's share. Will our men be willing to give up part of what they've won to treacherous enemies?"

"Men who *were* treacherous enemies," corrected Haakon gently. "But you also make sense. The new men won't share in the cargo we already have. They took no part in gaining it. For now they can be content with life, freedom, and a chance to regain their honor. If we do have another chance to raid, the gods will reward us with so much booty that every man will stagger under the weight of his share."

Bjorn felt a brief chill. Haakon had spoken with an

unmistakable ring of prophecy in his voice. Then the helmsman went on stubbornly. "What if the gods aren't so generous?"

"Then we'll take no chances. It would be foolish to risk losing more men or either ship. Far better to get home, fill both *Red Hawk* and *Wave Walker* with fighting men, and try again next spring. But I have hopes I didn't have this morning, now that our fortune seems to be changing." He went on briskly, "Let's leave the decision until we have both ships safe."

Bjorn nodded in agreement, then climbed up on the railing and dropped down to *Red Hawk*'s deck. If Haakon's luck really *was* turning after all this time, nothing could be more welcome. A Norseman feared a reputation for bad luck as much as a straw death in bed, and more than the swords of strong enemies. Such a reputation could reduce a chieftain to the level of a thrall—even a chieftain such as Haakon, who seemed to Bjorn fit to make a name that would last ten generations.

For a short journey in good weather, *Red Hawk*'s men were enough to handle both ships, so there was no delay in getting underway. The prisoners were bound and divided between the two ships. Bjorn took command of *Wave Walker*, while Haakon remained aboard *Red Hawk*. Then they hoisted sails and shaped a course toward the east.

Two hours later they raised a small island to the south. Another two hours was enough to take them into its rocky cove, where both ships could be safely grounded in water shallow enough for the men to wade ashore. Masses of driftwood and seaweed lay about on the coarse gravel beach, thrown there by the tide and now dry enough to fuel fires. The island itself was only a few miles long, but high and steep enough to be a solid barrier to storms from the west. Haakon wanted to deal with his prisoners on dry land. Also, he did not want to try sailing by night with his men divided between two ships, one of which was unfamiliar and in poor condition.

Haakon's men waded ashore, leading the bound prisoners or carrying sleeping gear, food, and weapons on their shoulders. Tents were unrolled and pitched, wood and seaweed piled up for campfires, sentries posted. The prisoners were led off to a place well away from the camp, still bound and escorted by three guards. The wounded and two of Haakon's men remained aboard each of the longships.

When the work of making camp was done, Haakon knew it was time to speak to the prisoners. Alone, he walked over to them and sent the guards away. Then he began asking questions of each man. Who was he? Where was he from? Why had he been aboard *Wave Walker*?

Haakon could roar like a bear when he had to. He could also speak gently and encouragingly to frightened or sullen men, sounding like a kindly uncle to warriors ten and twenty years older than he. Most of the prisoners spoke, sooner or later. Some of them poured their stories into Haakon's ear like ale from a jug. They were relieved not to have been killed outright and were happy to find someone apparently willing to listen without prejudging them.

Others grunted out only a few words, and Haakon took special care to remember their names. Their wits might still be numb from the shock of defeat and captivity. However, their sullenness might also hide secrets too shameful to confess or plans for treachery.

At Haakon's signal, Bjorn and the guards returned, bringing salt fish, bread, and water, then untying the prisoners' hands so they could eat. All the prisoners tore at the food like starving animals. Even if no one had admitted it, Haakon would have known that for a long time food was almost nonexistent aboard *Wave Walker*.

Short rations were only part of the story of *Wave Walker*'s unhappy voyage under the man known only as Leatherbreeches. It was a dreary tale of just about every misfortune Norsemen could suffer.

To begin with, their chief and captain had been called "Leatherbreeches" because he would tell no one his father's name. Was he a bastard or an outlaw whose life depended on anonymity? In either case, he was certainly a man eaten from within, both in mind and in body. He had the skills of a master sailor and a warrior, but he also had a madman's temper and a cough that twisted him like a snake and sometimes brought up blood. In years past he'd been known to fill his men's hands with silver in spite of these failings, so it did not seem entirely foolish to ship with him.

Wave Walker had sailed early in the year—too early, they learned within a few days. They met a storm that drove them onto the English coast; so violent was the blow that there seemed little chance they would ever get their ship to sea again. If the men had been certain they could desert safely, two thirds would have, at once.

Unfortunately, they didn't know where they were. They could be on a shore held by the Danes, who would treat them well. They could also be within reach of an earl of the English king, Alfred, who would torture or make slaves of those who didn't die by the sword. No one enjoyed the thought of putting out to sea again under Leatherbreeches, but they enjoyed even less the thought of falling into English hands.

"Someone must have cursed us and turned our wits," one man told Haakon. "Otherwise we'd have told Leatherbreeches straight out—'take us home!' We might have had to live with the reputation of being men who preferred a straw death in bed, but we'd have been living."

Haakon nodded. "Yes. Sometimes it takes a very brave man to go on living, knowing that fools might call him a coward." The man smiled uncertainly, pleased at Haakon's wise praise but not quite sure where it might lead. "Go on," Haakon said.

The luck of *Wave Walker,* her captain, and his men did not change. There was a hidden rock that nearly sank her, and another storm that rent the sail and cracked the mast. There was an English ship that looked like easy prey but fought like a bull walrus. Six Vikings were dead or dying before the English deck was clear, and then there was nothing aboard her worth taking. There were wild Pictish tribesmen who ambushed a landing party searching for water, so five more men never returned to the ship.

So it went, week after week, on the bad-luck, cursed cruise. Haakon began to feel that his own miserable fortune of the past summer was mild compared to what these men had suffered. If they were telling the truth, that is—but why shouldn't they? Besides, all told more or less the same story, however much or little each one said.

No one knew much about Gunnar Thorsten, the lean, blond poet who'd stayed removed from the fighting. He'd walked out of a mist one morning when they were ashore trying to catch some sheep in the west of England. The

bard had been half-naked, more than half-starved, his
beard and hair as tangled and stiff as a thorn hedge. But
he walked up to the sentries like a king. He had a verse
for every occasion and a well-wielded ax in a fight. Some
said he must have escaped from slavery among the English, but that was only a guess. For all anyone knew
about his past, Gunnar Thorsten might have sprung full-
grown from the earth.

The poet seemed trustworthy, but he was only one man
out of more than twenty able-bodied prisoners. There was
no time to lose, for Haakon had to win them over or at
least keep them safely quiet.

It took Haakon only a moment to decide what he should
offer the prisoners. It took him longer to choose words
that might make them accept his offer. To be sure, the
men had little choice: They could follow Haakon or die.
He did not want to hurl threats at them if he could avoid
it. That would only make them sullen, suspicious, and
ready for betrayal, which might doom both ships and all
aboard them.

Besides, now that he'd heard their story, Haakon found
these men worthy of respect—not honor or good sense,
perhaps, not when they'd followed so strange and twisted
a man as Leatherbreeches even into the worst sort of
shame. But there was courage in them, and a stubborn
refusal to let cruel bad luck beat them down.

He would like to have such men following him of their
own free will. Under a good leader, their courage might
win victories and help mend Haakon's own luck as well.
He'd been trying to sound more hopeful than he felt when
he'd talked to Bjorn about more successful raids with a

larger band of fighting men. But if it turned out that he'd spoken the truth . . .

Bjorn and the guards bound the prisoners' hands again, then Haakon sent his men away. When the others were gone, Haakon began walking up and down, feet crunching on the gravel just outside the light cast by the driftwood fire in the middle of the circle of prisoners. Slowly, words and phrases wove themselves into a pattern in his mind, like a fabric taking shape on a loom.

While Haakon was lost in thought, one of his men brought food and slipped away without disturbing him. Haakon was roused to the world around him by nearly stumbling over the wooden platter. He squatted down, ate a few mouthfuls, then realized that in spite of all the day's work, he wasn't hungry. He rose, combed his beard with his fingers, and strode into the circle of light around the prisoners' fire.

Every face turned toward Haakon. Some still looked sullen, but most looked merely uncertain. They had no more secrets from Haakon. He'd learned too much about who they were and what they'd done. Now they were probably wondering what he was going to do with them; he could do anything he wanted, and here on this lonely night-shrouded island neither gods nor men could stop him.

Haakon said nothing, but only piled another armload of driftwood on the fire. It sank down for a moment, then blazed higher as the wood caught. Haakon brushed cinders from his leather jerkin, put his hands on his hips, and spoke.

"Men of Leatherbreeches and *Wave Walker*," he began, "you attacked my ship under the peace shield. This was treachery, hateful to both gods and men. By that treachery you have given up your honor, and your lives are mine to take." He was silent for a moment, to let the harsh facts sink into the men's minds.

Then he said softly, "Yet I do not want your lives. I want to give you a chance to win back your honor." Most of the men in the circle must have been holding their breaths. The hissing sighs all around the fire sounded like a nest of adders.

Haakon's voice was loud now. "You have all suffered enough. You have endured the madness of Leatherbreeches, foul weather, the swords of the English and the spears of the Picts, thirst and hunger, the loss of comrades, and now defeat and captivity. Your captain is dead, and half your comrades along with him. I have no further quarrel with any of you, unless you give me one." He raised one arm and swept it in a gesture that took in the whole circle of prisoners.

"Swear to follow me as captain and chief, aboard ship and in battle, until this year's voyaging ends. Swear by Odin, by Thor, and by whatever else you hold most precious. Swear this oath, and I will swear to regard each of you as one of my men.

"You will be in no more danger than you have been. Less, I suspect, for I am not Leatherbreeches and I will not lead you where he would have led. You will have more hope of good luck and reward. Two ships together can do much if their men know how to fight. You know how, and I think you will agree that so do the men of *Red Hawk*."

Several captives laughed at Haakon's statement. It was the first laughter from these men since the battle, and it served to break the tension. Haakon grinned. "I do not promise that you will leave me staggering under the weight of your loot. I do promise that when you step ashore and leave me, you will have your honor back. I will say nothing of what Leatherbreeches's men did, and neither will the men of *Red Hawk*. You will leave as free men, with the chance to do as well as fate permits."

There was no laughter this time, only a sustained, brooding silence, which prompted Haakon to wonder if the men had understood him. Then a one-eyed man with a scraggly beard streaked with gray spoke up.

"Haakon, how can you promise us that all your men will keep quiet about—what we've done?" he said bluntly. "You give the orders, but ale can make men forget them."

Haakon nodded. "I give the orders, but what happens after that is in your hands. If you keep your oaths and are good comrades in battle and storm, my men will tell no tales. Who would wish to blacken the name of a man who's fought beside him? But if you give them reason to talk of the wretched, treacherous, useless fools we took on from *Wave Walker*, then they will do so, ale or no ale."

This produced another silence. It also dragged on, until a small dark man who spoke Norse with a strange accent asked the inevitable question.

"If we do not swear to go with you—if then—what happens?"

Haakon shrugged. "As I said, you have been punished enough. I will not have your blood on my hands, nor will I lead men who have sworn oaths out of fear. Yet I can hardly take you with me if you do not swear. I will leave you your ship and all her gear, your swords, and your

clothing. Then my men and I will sail away and your fate
will be in your own hands."

"And you—you will not be quiet, about us?"

"Why should I be?"

Silence again. Haakon's promise to leave the men and
their ship on the island might seem like no more than a
delayed sentence of death. It was not, and he expected the
men would realize this. With enough hard work and luck,
they could certainly sail *Wave Walker* to some Norse land.
Then they would be safe, unless they met someone who'd
heard from Haakon's men that the survivors of Leatherbreeches's band were outlaws.

Even if the men would not join him, Haakon didn't
want their blood. He would merely leave them to gods
and men who might show little mercy, and to the sea,
which never showed any at all.

This silence did not last as long as the ones before. A
ripple of movement and another hissing sigh seemed to
run around the circle of prisoners. The one-eyed man
raised his bound hands toward Haakon, who stepped
forward and cut the ropes at the man's wrists and ankles.
Then the man knelt in front of Haakon, put his hands into
the chieftain's, and said in a loud, steady voice:

"I, Knut Aleksson, called the One-Eye, swear by Odin
and Thor and by my hope of a good death to follow
Haakon Olesson in all that he does and to be one of his
men, until death takes me or he makes me free of this
oath."

One by one, each prisoner knelt before the chieftain
and joined Knut in taking the oath. One by one, Haakon
cut the bindings of each prisoner. At first Haakon wondered what he should do with anyone who refused. Then

he saw that none would. He had struck something deep in these men—their honor, their practical wisdom, perhaps only their hope of loot—and they were coming forward willingly.

At last all twenty-three men had knelt before Haakon and sworn their oaths. By now it was completely dark, and the fire needed more wood. Haakon piled it on and waited until the flames danced and whirled in the rising wind. Haakon could hear the booming rumble of the surf on the rocky shore.

The wind was not very strong, yet Haakon felt a chill, as though he were standing naked on an ice floe in the cold North. A strange knowledge came to him that this oath-taking was the moment when his life and fate would take a new turn, one he could not even imagine. There was a *presence* in the wind, a presence that spoke to him as clearly as any of the prisoners—now men who had pledged him their lives.

If he listened, would this presence tell him what the new turning might be? Haakon waited for a long moment, half-hoping to hear the answer in the wind. Then he laughed at the notion. A man did not conjure from the gods answers they were unwilling to give. He would wait for them to answer in their own time, and meanwhile he did his best with the knowledge and the skills he already had.

All eyes were on Haakon as he rested one hand on the hilt of his sword and pressed the other fist to his heart. "By Odin and Thor, by my own honor, by this sword I bear, and by my hope of avenging my brother's and sisters' deaths and my father's shame, I swear that all those who have sworn to follow me shall have all I owe to any man who follows me. They shall be to me as those of *Red Hawk* have been. No word against their honor will ever pass my lips. If I break the least part of this oath, may I fail in all that I attempt, may my own honor be swept away, and may my death be cold and shameful."

Haakon was barely finished when one-eyed Knut sprang to his feet. "Haakon!" he cheered. "Haakon!"

The others also jumped up, pounding fists on chests and thighs and stamping their feet. "Haakon!" they shouted. "Haakon!" They would have been beating their weapons against their shields if they'd had them. The chanting rose until it drowned out the wind and drew echoes from the cliffs.

At last the ragged chorus of "Haakon!" died away. In the silence, Haakon felt the eerie presence more strongly than before. Suddenly it became the most important force in the world; he felt compelled to get away from the fire and these men and be alone in the darkness, alone with the wind. In solitude, Haakon might be able to understand what the presence was trying to tell him.

"Get some sleep," he said to the men. "The night will be gone soon enough, and there's work to be done on the ships in the morning." He passed out of the circle and headed out toward the darkness beyond the firelight.

He was barely outside the circle of light when a figure loomed up before him. His hand was on his sword hilt before he recognized Bjorn.

"So you've won them over, Haakon. I was listening, and certainly Odin guided your tongue and their hearts."

"Yes," was all that Haakon could say in answer. After a moment, he said, "See that their gear is brought ashore from *Wave Walker.* I'm going to climb inland and look for fresh water."

"In the darkness? I thought we—"

"It's a clear night, and sleep doesn't appeal to me."

"The idea of searching this island for you if you fall down a cliff isn't appealing either," said Bjorn. He forced a smile. "Very well, but take care, jarl. I think your luck has turned today, but I don't see hawk's wings sprouting from your back to fly you from mountaintop to mountaintop."

Haakon laughed and gripped the helmsman by both shoulders. "I'll take care." As he walked away he was conscious of Bjorn looking after him for a moment, probably with a frown on his face. Then the darkness was all around him as he began to climb the rocky slope leading inland.

III

Haakon felt the darkness leap on him as if it were alive and hungry. His sense of balance told him that the slope under his feet was growing rapidly steeper. Small stones crunched under his boots, larger ones rolled free and crashed and clattered away into the night. Several times he had to drop to his hands and knees to keep from slipping and tumbling after the rocks.

As he climbed, he bore off to the right. In that direction, so his memory told him, lay a ragged gap between two of the rocky hills around the cove. That gap might lead him safely inland. Elsewhere the hills jutted up rugged and steep so only a man with the hawk's wings Bjorn spoke of could pass over them, even in daylight.

And what if the gap led nowhere, or to a fatal plunge down a cliff? Somehow he did not expect to meet great danger on the other side of the gap in the cliffs. The presence in the wind had not called him out into the night alone to kill him or to play tricks. He could not say why he felt it to be so, but he did know that the feeling was strong inside him, and it grew stronger as he climbed higher.

Haakon reached the gap. It was so narrow that three brave men could have held it against an army. On either side, vertical cliffs towered higher than a tall tree. They shut off every bit of starlight from the path ahead and left it in a darkness that seemed not of this world. Haakon's eyes were normally sharp, able to pierce the night when most men saw nothing. But now he felt he was looking into a place the gods had cursed with perpetual darkness, as though no light had ever shone there or ever would. It was difficult for Haakon to keep from feeling that if he moved on he, too, would become a creature of darkness for all time.

It was also impossible for him to think of stopping, now that he'd come this far. He threw back his head and laughed, his beard whipping in the wind, ignoring the way the rock walls hurled back the echo of his laughter. With his right hand he drew his sword and lowered its tip to the ground; with his left hand he drew his dagger and held it point-out in front of him. Now it would be hard for him to blunder into any traps or over any cliffs. As surely as he would have moved along the rolling deck in a storm, Haakon strode forward into the darkness.

The rock was solid underfoot and sloped gently downward. The passage twisted back and forth like the trail of a snake, sometimes turning so sharply that Haakon's weapons scraped on a solid rock wall rising suddenly in front of him. At times Haakon could have sworn the passage doubled back on itself, so that in three minutes he was moving in three different directions. The feeling was growing in him that this island did not follow the laws ruling the rest of the world.

Once the passage led him into a tunnel that had been riven through solid rock, a tunnel that was as long as a ship. Haakon knew the tunnel was real, because he reached out and felt the walls on either side. He reached up and felt the ceiling only inches above his head. Whether this was a tunnel carved out by wind and water or by human hands and tools, he could not hope to learn in this darkness.

Beyond the tunnel the passage was narrower still. Haakon found he could not stretch his arms out to their full length on either side. The air was still, cold, and damp, but high overhead the wind blew, calling out insistently. The wind's voice no longer called Haakon onward, but cried out like the ghosts of men murdered and left unburied, shrieking for vengeance. This lonely island, seemingly uninhabited, far from the world—he'd never seen a better place for treachery or secret murder.

Haakon knew more about treachery than he cared to. Another man's treachery had set the course of Haakon's life: Twenty years earlier, Haakon's father, Ole Ketilsson, and his wife, Sigrid, lived peacefully on a riverbank steading in Ireland. For many years there was stronger friend-

ship between Norse and Irish along that river than anywhere else in Ireland.

Then, a Viking jarl named Olaf Haraldsson ended the
calm with an unexpected and savage attack. Haraldsson
wanted Ole's alliance in his quest to become ruler of all
the Norse in Ireland. If he could not have Ole's friendship, he wanted Ole's land. Ole refused him both and
prepared to defend what was his. But his men were few
and used to peace, and his ships were worm-eaten.

Ole and his wife Sigrid awoke one night to find Olaf's
warriors swarming onto the steading. The battle that
followed left Olaf unscathed, but so many of his men were
dead or hurt that he had to retreat. Ole himself had a
great wound in the thigh, and most of his people were
dead or hurt past fighting. Ole knew that Olaf would
attack again before Ole could obtain aid from his wife's kin
or from his own kin in Norway. There was nothing to do
but admit that this battle was lost, and return to Norway.
Ole and Sigrid buried their son Thorgrim and daughter
Asa. Then Ole loaded his surviving family and his silver
aboard the soundest of his ships and put out to sea.

On the voyage back to the Trondelag, the older daughter died off the Orkneys, and Ole's wound showed no sign
of healing. By the time they reached home, it was clear he
would not fight Olaf again. Soon after that, it was clear he
would not travel again either, at least not in this world.

Knowing this, Ole Ketilsson fought his last and hardest
battle to make sure that Sigrid would be left in peace and
his surviving son, a child named Haakon, would receive a
proper inheritance. By the time that battle was finished,
the silver he'd brought from Ireland was nearly gone, but
he'd done his work. Enough men had sworn oaths to Ole,

promising that his holdings would be divided lawfully between his widow and his son.

Then Ole died. His name was as yet unavenged, and the treacherous Olaf Haraldsson was often in the darkest thoughts of Sigrid. She had sworn Haakon Olesson to either avenge his father or to die trying.

Olaf now ruled as jarl over the stolen lands, and he grew fat from all the booty of his dishonor. Haakon had never forgotten his oath of revenge for his brother's death and his father's shame, even though his distraught mother had often accused him of it to his face. Haakon would choose his own time and place to strike Olaf, but only when he could sail to Ireland with a strong fleet. Meanwhile, Haakon questioned every man he met who'd come from Ireland. There was little that Olaf Haraldsson had done in the last seven years that Haakon had not learned.

Haakon walked on through the darkness, his mind so full of the past that he didn't notice when the rock walls vanished from either side of him. He only knew that suddenly the wind blew harder, and he was in the open, standing at the bottom of a great bowllike hollow in the rock. The rim of the bowl was studded with jagged boulders twice the height of a man. Here the wind whipped wildly, cold and whining. The strange presence was still with Haakon, but it was no longer just a wordless voice in the wind, calling him on. Now Haakon had an overpowering sense that it was watching him. He tensed and gripped his weapons.

Haakon crouched low, sword and dagger ready. He turned in a complete circle, his eyes searching the darkness and the rocks. If enemies were watching, they were so well hidden no human eye could find them.

Haakon suddenly knew he had stepped beyond the limits of his world. A gray wool mist was rising out of the rock, climbing halfway up the walls of the passage, then falling back. The mist spread over Haakon like a shroud, undisturbed in spite of the wind. Then it fell away from him and all sensation vanished.

Was this death? He felt chilled and uncertain. It was not a warrior's death in battle nor even a straw death in bed. Was it a death conjured up for him by evil spirits who'd led him here, deceived him as they drew him farther out into the darkness? Anger rose within him. This was a foul death, not worthy of a warrior, and it would leave Olaf Haraldsson alive and his crimes unavenged.

Rage stopped the breath in Haakon's throat. The blood roared in his head. His mouth opened to curse whatever had led him here.

Then a voice spoke clear words.

"Haakon Olesson, this is not your death. For you, this is a new beginning."

The voice was in his mind, but it was as alive as if it had spoken into his ears. It was loud, round, the voice of a man who for many years had been shouting commands over storms and battle. It was also a boldly confident voice, the voice of a man who finds nothing strange or awesome in the world.

Haakon could not have been more surprised if the earth had opened up and swallowed him. He stiffened and raised his weapons. Then the mist drew back from the passage in the rock, and Haakon saw shapes taking form at its mouth: a broad-chested, bandy-legged man with a thick, red beard and curly, reddish hair shot with gray. A four-wheeled cart, its body richly carved as if intended for

a king. Two goats were harnessed to the cart, goats the
size of mules, with horns of shining silver and eyes of a
blazing green that Haakon could never have imagined
possible. The man raised his right hand. There was a
hammer in it. Haakon felt shock course through him. He
now knew who had called him to this place tonight!

Thor! Thor Odinsson, himself! Thor, wielder of the
hammer Mjolnir, slayer of giants, fisher for the World
Serpent, lord of the thunder, patron of sailors and travel-
ers. A friendly god if one made the proper sacrifices and
broke no oath sworn by him. Haakon had always shown
the Thunderer proper respect, yet now he could not keep
back his fear.

He was not ashamed of the fear. When a man stands
alone in the windy darkness face to face with Thor—

"You swore an oath that no man would put fear into you,
Haakon Olesson," said Thor. He seemed amused.

"I am not forsworn," replied Haakon. "You are no man,
even if you are not Thor but a deceiver."

The answer to that was a great, deep roar of laughter,
whirling the mist about like a strong gust of wind. Haakon
smiled. The laughter did not prove that what he saw was
truly Thor, but it left him with a new feeling that there
was no danger here for him. But—if no danger, then
what?

Silence. Haakon stole another glance around him. The
reins of the goats shimmered like rainbows, but in colors
no rainbow ever showed. Stags were carved on Mjolnir's
handle, and the hubs of the cart's wheels were shaped like
the heads of boars. He heard Thor's voice in his mind
again.

"Haakon, this is not your death. No. Instead, it is a

turning in your fortunes, which you began yourself with the victory over *Wave Walker*. That was your work, and it pleased us."

"I did not do it only to please the gods."

There was another long silence, then:

"We know that. But you showed much wisdom and justice in dealing with your prisoners. These qualities are rare among men. A man who shows them as you have is fit to serve the gods."

"When a warrior's death finds me, I will be honored to serve them."

"You do not understand, Haakon Olesson. You will be our servant even while you walk the earth as a living man."

"How?"

"The world is full of matters where a man such as you is needed. Many men have done wrong and need to be set right. That will be your work."

"Do you ask me to fight the Norns?" The Norns, Keepers of Fate, ruled both gods and men. If this was indeed Thor asking him to go against them, the god was not speaking understandably. If this was a dream, it was madness. Thor spoke:

"Norns will rule as they have always ruled. You will do nothing against them, indeed nothing we could not have done ourselves. But Mjolnir does not have a light touch, and among men sometimes all a matter needs is a light but well-aimed touch. Was our hammer needed to strike down Leatherbreeches or to find a way to save the honor of his foolish men? No."

"I understand."

"You will know our wishes when they come to you. Do not fear that we will ever leave you groping in darkness."

"Like the darkness of this island?"

Thor laughed. "Well said. And in time..." His voice died, and he raised one arm in a sharp, commanding gesture. Suddenly there was no more mist, but instead a soft, golden light, which seemed to emanate from every direction. Before, the island had been a place of darkness; now it was a place of such glorious light that darkness might never have been.

Out of the golden light a picture took shape: a vast hall, so great and so wide that it could have held ten longships. The pillars on either side were blue stone, the floor seemed all of silver, and the roof was concealed behind a veil of golden mist. Wondrous music floated out of that mist—horns, drums, harps, all played so exquisitely that Haakon felt close to weeping for joy.

Along the hall were tables and benches, carved of a wood so highly polished it seemed to glow. Warriors in feast-day robes sat on benches all along the tables. Their swords and helmets glittered by their sides. They drank ale and mead from horns that floated in the air before them. They ate great slabs of pork from golden platters that replenished themselves as fast as they were emptied. Among the warriors Haakon saw tall, fair-haired women with terrible beauty in their faces. They were robed for feasting but bore shields and spears.

Valhalla! This was Valhalla! This was a vision of the hall of the gods, where heroes slain in battle went to fight and feast until the end of all things. The robed women were

the Valkyries, the Choosers of the Slain, and now he saw
that their eyes were a blue so deep it was almost purple.

"Yes, Valhalla. Are you worthy of a place there?"

"If I escape a straw death, yes."

"No. Only by serving us will you win a place among the
heroes of Valhalla. Serve us, and you shall attain Valhalla
no matter where death comes to you." Thor laughed. "It is
better to bring a brave and honorable man to Valhalla,
even though he's died a straw death, than to bring some
fool who found death in battle because he forgot to tighten
his helmet strap."

If this was a dream, it was indeed a strange mixture of
madness and wisdom. But if it was a true sight sent by
Thor and was truly a message from him . . .

"I only know how to swear *by* a god, not *to* one," said
Haakon. "Is it enough to say that as long as I am not asked
to go against Fate, I shall serve the gods as best I can?"

"It is enough, Haakon. Your newfound, good fortune
will go on. It will continue until you have avenged all of
Olaf Haraldsson's crimes, until the end of your life. If you
show the wisdom and justice you have displayed today,
that life will be long and rich.

"Be a friend to kings who deserve your friendship and
accept from them whatever rewards they offer. But never
accept a crown or reach out for one yourself. The moment
a crown touches your brow, your fortunes will turn for the
worse, and your life thereafter will be short. My father,
Odin, calls some men to be kings, but you are not among
them. You have another task.

"Go from this place, then, Haakon Olesson. Know that
your fortunes have turned, and take with you—this gift of
Thor."

At the last word, Mjolnir, the hammer, was suddenly high in the god's hand. It flashed in a mighty arc and crashed down on the rock at Thor's feet. The solid stone split and intense light spilled out, raw, blazing, golden light that almost blinded Haakon. He watched through narrowed eyes as the crack in the rock widened and golden vapor poured out, mixing with the mist. The crack slowly filled with fiercely glowing liquid rock. He saw the lava take shape—a battle-ax, a golden ax so long that most men would have needed two hands to wield it.

The ax took form until it seemed to float in the liquid rock like a leaf on a pond. Again Mjolnir flashed down, and this time thunder crashed and a pillar of golden light towered higher than the mast of a ship. Haakon heard the deafening thunder with his ears as well as his mind, and the echoes rolled around the rocks for a long time before they finally died away.

When silence came, Thor pointed Mjolnir at the golden ax. It lay with its handle toward Haakon, on a patch of rock that had been gray and now was blackened and charred.

"It is cunning work, Haakon. Take this ax, and you will see that it is a good gift, a gift fit for a servant of the gods."

Haakon slowly stepped to within reach of the ax and hesitantly bent down. An insistent voice in his mind warned him that now the trick of the evil spirits would finally reveal itself: The ax would sear his hands to blackened stumps and leave him a beggar to the end of his days. But another voice said that now he would wake from his dreams and find that he gripped only a stone or a piece of wood.

He closed his mind to both voices and gripped the ax

with both hands. The handle was warm, as it might have been if a man had been holding it for a few minutes. The warmth flowed from his hands into his arms and shoulders, giving Haakon a sense of immense strength. Runes that Haakon could not read were carved along it, and the thong was tough red leather. But it was the blade that was a marvel, for it was golden. He raised it over his head and then swung it with his right hand in a great circle. The hiss of air had a comforting familiarity about it. The balance was the best he'd ever felt. Its makers might be dwarfs, or gods, or beings for whom there was no name— whoever they were, they knew their work as no one else knew it.

Haakon raised the ax in salute. He saw Thor's smile. Then the god leaped into his cart and raised his hammer. Thunder crashed down again, so loud that Haakon was tempted to clap his hands over his ears. He stood with the ax raised as Thor, his cart, and the goats vanished. A mighty gale howled through the passage where they had been standing. Lightning bolts shot through the sky, and the winds of the unearthly storm scattered the mist and picked up Haakon, reeling and hurling him across the rocky bowl like a child's doll. His head smashed into the rock. Again he saw golden fire, luminous bows, axes, gods, Valkyries, and Valhalla. Then darkness came, and nothing else mattered to Haakon—servant of Thor, and wielder of the golden ax.

IV

Bjorn doubted Haakon's tale about why he was going inland, but did not want a useless quarrel. When Haakon made a decision, neither friends nor enemies could persuade him to change it.

It was all very well to tell himself that a quarrel would have been useless, perhaps even dangerous if it showed the prisoners that *Red Hawk*'s two leaders were divided. It was comforting to say that there was no danger inland that Haakon couldn't face. It was even possible to say that Haakon was going to meet a Norn who waited for him among the cold rocks of the island, and no man should stand between him and his fate.

It was so easy to say all those things that Bjorn said them over and over again as the fires burned down to coals and were piled high again with driftwood. It was also difficult not to feel that he was trying to argue away his own failure in not being able to stop Haakon. By the predawn hours, he couldn't drive away a recurring picture of Haakon's body lying broken and stiffening at the bottom of some cliff.

Yet, what could be done before dawn? In the darkness searchers would be so nearly blind that they'd be risking the same fate that might have overtaken Haakon. And who would be sent to search? Bjorn was not yet ready to trust

Wave Walker's men alone with an injured Haakon; nor did
he expect them to keep their oaths if they learned he was
dead or missing. If he sent only *Red Hawk*'s men, he'd be
leaving too few behind to watch *Wave Walker*'s crew. If he
sent men from both ships, the ones from *Red Hawk* would
have to be sure they found Haakon first.

The simplest thing would be to bind them all hand and
foot again and leave only a few *Red Hawk* men behind.
But if some among *Wave Walker*'s crew still felt bound by
their oaths, wouldn't they take this as a mortal insult?

Bjorn sighed. He would get no sleep tonight. Better sit
down and use the wakeful hours to solve some of the
dilemmas he faced. If it was Haakon's fate not to come
back, Bjorn would need answers by dawn, when everyone
would turn to him.

He was looking for a place to sit when he sensed
someone standing behind him. His hand was on his sword
hilt as he turned sharply to face one-eyed Knut Aleksson
from *Wave Walker*. Then both hands dropped to Bjorn's
sides as he thought of Father Odin, who had sacrificed one
eye for the gift of runes and who often walked among men,
disguising all of his godhood except the missing eye.

Knut laughed.

"What's so funny?"

"I am not Odin."

It did not reassure Bjorn to hear Knut guess his thoughts.
The helmsman grew uneasy; as if they were their own
masters, his feet carried him two steps backward.

Knut laughed again. "No, truly. I know what you think
because a hundred men and women have also thought it.
Most of them spoke it as well." He put a hand to the

leather patch over his empty socket. "This does not make people feel easy toward me."

Bjorn managed to smile. "So you did not give up that eye to learn runes?"

"No. I gave it to learn the use of a sword. It was bad luck for my teacher, and maybe worse luck for me. My father thought it was an omen and wanted me to be made a priest of Odin and serve the god all my days."

"You refused?"

"I could not refuse with words. My father only listened to what he wanted to hear. I knew a chieftain looking for fighting men and went to him. When his ship sailed west, I was in her crew.

"That was twenty years ago, and I do not know even now if I took from Odin something that was rightfully his. My luck comes and goes. Right now, I think it has come again, and I will do my best to see that it does not slip away." He crossed his arms on his chest. "You think Haakon has been gone too long?"

Bjorn said simply, "Yes."

"I think so, too. But in this darkness, when we do not know the island, can we do anything before dawn?"

"No. If Haakon is alive, he won't die of this cold before morning. If he's dead, we won't help him by killing more of our own men trying to find him."

Knut nodded. "If he is dead, I will swear a new oath to you. I will not follow you against the English, but I will do anything and fight anyone to get us all safely home."

Bjorn's first thought was common sense. *If Haakon isn't coming back, it would be useless to do anything but salvage what luck we have left and use it to get home.*

"I won't ask anyone to go raiding without Haakon,"

Bjorn said. "If I'll have your voice among *Wave Walker's* men—"

"You'll have that, Bjorn Karlsson, and my sword beside yours if it's needed."

"I thank you."

When Knut was gone, Bjorn realized it would have been better if he'd gone to the man first and made Knut follow his lead. Knut thought faster, though. Bjorn realized he might not need to guard his back against the one-eyed man, but he might need to guard against his becoming chief over the two ships if Haakon didn't return.

Haakon awoke when the last stars and the first light of dawn were in the sky together. He forced himself to move, though he ached as if a herd of cattle had trampled across him. He sat up slowly while life, blood, and warmth crept back into his arms and legs. His senses returned, and so did his memory of the night and his dreams.

He found it easier to call it a dream. *No, it's not just easier. I don't want to think it might have been something real.* He remembered that he had known fear during the dream. Now he found he was afraid again. He looked around at the rocks and was happy to see no signs of where the molten lava had bubbled up beneath the earth. Then with a wrenching shock, he saw the ax. It stood with the handle leaning against a boulder. The low sun flashed light off its golden blade.

The sight of the ax jerked Haakon to his feet and pushed him beyond fear. *The ax is real. How much else of last night was real?* He stared wide-eyed. What if he tried to touch it?

Haakon wouldn't have been surprised or even particularly unhappy if the ax vanished in a puff of smoke when he gripped it. Instead, it rose smoothly in his fist as if it were a living thing eager to obey him. The metal was warm to his touch, even though there was no logical explanation for the phenomenon. The warmth flowed into his hands and arms from the ax, rather than the other way around.

The metal head was thicker than was usual, and when he tapped a stone against it, it did not ring quite like the axheads Haakon knew. The golden color was also unusual. It was not a thin layer of gold leaf beaten onto the axhead, easily scratched or scraped off. From the color, Haakon would have said the axhead was bronze, but it was harder than any blade he'd ever encountered. It couldn't be gold, because that precious metal was too soft.

As a weapon, the ax was magnificent, a masterpiece about which songs were sung. It was beautifully balanced, and in spite of the weight, Haakon found he could make it fly about his head like a bird. As the ax danced, he danced, too, until he'd worked the last of the chill and the aches out of his legs.

The handle was of a close-grained reddish wood Haakon did not recognize, highly polished except in two places where it was bound with sharkskin. The skins were positioned to give a perfect two-handed grip. The ax was light enough to be used one-handed if necessary, but a two-handed grip would make it a better weapon. With two hands he could strike harder, more accurately, and with less effort. But did he have to worry about fatigue? This ax seemed to supply its own strength, or at the very least, replenish Haakon's.

Haakon remembered Thor's words, the ax was "cunning

work." Man or god or whoever else the smith might be, the maker of the ax was a master of his craft. It would be deadly in battle, and the men it slew—the enemies of Haakon Olesson or the enemies of Thor and the other lords of Valhalla—they would be just as dead.

It was time to be on his way back to the ships, with the ax and a tale to explain it: *"I went farther than I intended, then I decided to stop rather than get lost trying to return in the darkness. I found a cave big enough to get me out of the wind. I fell asleep there and had a strange dream: The rear of the cave was brightly lit. When I woke I went to the rear of the cave and found the ax half-buried in the earth."*

That seemed good enough, although he wondered if his face was that of a man who'd done nothing during the night but sleep in a cave and dream strange dreams.

Before he was halfway back to the ships, Haakon met the men searching for him.

The first thing he asked for when he returned to the beach was something to eat and drink. He emptied two full mugs of ale and half of a third before the food came, then made two bowls of porridge and another of salt meat vanish as if they'd been dropped down a well. Then he finished the ale, combed his beard, and for the first time seemed to notice the men standing around him.

Haakon's tale was simple, and Bjorn was sure that although most of the men believed it, Haakon was not telling the whole truth. Gradually the others drifted away, talking among themselves about the marvelous battle-ax, leaving the two chiefs alone. Bjorn waited until everyone was out of hearing, then he spoke.

"Are you sure the ax wasn't grave goods?"

Haakon shook his head. "No, but if it was a grave, it certainly wasn't Norse."

"It isn't only Norse ghosts who take vengeance for robbed graves."

Haakon seemed about to shrug away Bjorn's words, then looked at his friend more closely. What he saw seemed to change his mind.

"I didn't tell everything about my dream."

"Did a spirit show you the ax?"

"More than that: Thor Odinsson—or something in his shape—called the ax up out of the earth on a flood of molten stone. Yes, it's the truth, by my father's memory! Does that sound like something I'd dream in a grave barrow, with the dead man's ghost still guarding his weapons?"

"No. Though I've heard of ghosts taking strange shapes . . . The men'll be asking more about that ax, though. It's a strange one, and—"

"Tell me something I can't see with my own eyes," said Haakon. His smile took some of the edge from the words. "Bjorn, when did you last sleep?"

"I—" Bjorn found he could either speak or keep his legs from trembling with fatigue, but not both. He had steered or fought all day, then stayed awake all night.

"Go drink some ale and get some sleep, old friend. I didn't have a soft bed or a warm one, but I did sleep last night. What about you?"

Bjorn managed to laugh, but before he turned away he remembered Knut One-Eye. Haakon had to be told about the man. He got through his story, but he had to sit down to do it.

"You said exactly the right words, Bjorn," said Haakon. "It did no harm to have him come to you, either."

"He'll be able to say it was his idea."

"True. But he left the power in your hands to accept or turn aside the idea of searching for me. You accepted the idea, but for the light of dawn, and that simply proves you're not a fool. It's not a sign of weakness. Knut isn't a fool, either. I'd like to learn more about him. Somewhere he's learned far more than I'd·expect of someone willing to follow Leatherbreeches."

Bjorn nodded and rubbed his eyes. Haakon bent over and pulled him to his feet. "Go and get some sleep, in Odin's name. It's you who'll be falling down and breaking bones if you don't."

"I—oh, very well." Vaguely Bjorn heard Haakon calling two men to come and help steer the helmsman to a safe bed.

Steer the helmsman. Bjorn would have laughed if he'd had the strength.

By the time Haakon left Bjorn, the day's work on the longships was already beginning. Mauls thudded, adzes scraped, and walrus-hide ropes groaned as they were tested. Curses flew when some of the ropes broke and spilled the men testing them onto the stones of the beach. Both crews seemed to be following the orders of Snorri Longfoot, *Red Hawk*'s carpenter. Men said that Snorri was born with a chisel in his hands and was weaned on wood chips.

As Haakon watched the ships, Gunnar Thorsten hailed him formally from the deck of *Wave Walker*.

"Haakon Darkbeard! I would speak with you."

"I will hear you."

Gunnar waded ashore, then led Haakon up onto the lower slope of the hill behind the beach. Gunnar found a rock high enough so his tall frame would be comfortably accommodated. Then he seemed to withdraw into his own thoughts. Haakon wondered if Gunnar was composing more poetry, then looked at his grim face again. Gunnar's thoughts were not on anything as pleasant as poetry.

"Haakon," the poet said abruptly. "Are we going to make raid before we return home? If we are, have you chosen where you'll make it?"

"I'll answer the first question: Yes. Before I answer the second, I'll ask you one: Why do you want to know?"

"If you haven't chosen, I want to suggest a place."

"Where?"

"The castle of Earl Edmund Oswainsson, where I was a slave."

The poet neither met Haakon's stare nor tried to avoid it. He was distantly lost in memories. His hands were still clasped over his knees, but now so tightly that the knuckles stood out white, like knots on a branch.

"Trusting you is one thing," Haakon said. "Making your vengeance my work is something else."

"I'm not a fool," said Gunnar. "The vengeance I'm thinking of needs men and ships like yours, but it will also pay well. Do I interest you, Haakon?"

"You may interest me. Tell me more."

"Will you swear that you will either follow the course I show you or keep silent about what I've told you?"

"If any of it shames you, certainly."

Gunnar shook his head angrily. His long, pale hair flew about his ears. "No. Not shame. There's shame enough that I'm still alive. I should have taken a sword and fought

my way to a warrior's death. If you can't use what I tell
you now, you may want to use it on a day when you have
more men. No one else should know until then."

"And if I don't want to use it at all?"

"Then I'll say nothing against you, but I will go to
another chief. One who will use what I tell him to make
himself rich and give me vengeance on Edmund of the
Ram's Head." His face turned from red to white and
flushed red again as he spoke. Then he suddenly laughed.
"Now, before you command me to, I'll stop talking in
riddles and tell you what you need to know."

Gunnar was a poet, but he could also tell a plain tale
swiftly. He'd been stranded on the English coast along
with four other men from the ship of Eldred Thick-Belly,
after a quarrel with Eldred over the division of booty from
a raid.

Gunnar had been captured and was a slave for two years
in Earl Edmund's castle on the cape called the Ram's
Head on the coast of the Irish Sea. No doubt he could
have been treated worse; he was alive, while some of his
fellow slaves were dead. However, there is nothing in
being a slave to nourish a man's pride, even if his body
survives.

The earl himself was away in King Alfred's service for
more than half of each year. His three sons were sometimes with him, sometimes at home, and nearly always
quarreling. All of the sons had cruel streaks in them, and
the servants and slaves would have been constantly scourged
and maltreated if it hadn't been for the earl's daughter,
Rosamund.

"Rosamund? Isn't that a Frankish name?"

"It might well be. Her mother, who died a few years

back, was a Frankish lady, from the Seine Valley up toward Paris. Some in the castle said Rosamund was all her child, while the sons were all their father's."

Whether this was true or not, the travels of the sons left Rosamund mistress of the castle from the age of fourteen. What peace and order there was existed mostly by her work. The few kind words Gunnar and the other slaves received came from her alone.

"I don't think even the Christians' lord, Christ, will save that family when Rosamund marries Harud Olafsson. That was why I was determined to escape when I did. With Rosamund gone to Ireland, it would have been flee or die at the hands of those misbegotten mongrels of brothers.

"I pity the lady. She'll not be happy in her marriage. Harud has already buried two wives, and they say he beat the second one to death while he was drunk." He laughed grimly. "If he tries such tricks with Rosamund, he'll find a knife between his ribs the first time he takes his eyes off her. I don't know if that will save her. It is said that Harud Olafsson has the evil eye and cannot be wounded in the manner of ordinary men."

"Is she beautiful?" Haakon did not know why he asked this question.

"Not really. Oh, she's fair, and there's plenty of flesh on her in the right places, but I've seen many better."

Haakon found that he was disappointed and took out that disappointment on Gunnar. "I've heard enough of your story. I know why you want vengeance. I warrant that you deserve it. Now tell me why I should help you."

It seemed that when Earl Edmund was away, so were most of his fighting men. At that time, forty or fifty good warriors, helped by surprise, darkness, and a man who knew the country and the castle could beat down the remaining defenders and loot it thoroughly. They would do a good night's work, too. Gunnar's eyes were aflame.

"I've seen gold vessels as big as a man's head, and an ivory drinking horn set with jewels," he said. "If Rosamund's dowry hasn't been paid out, there should also be two or three chests of coins somewhere in the castle. It probably hasn't been paid," he added. "If the earl's not known as Edmund the Miser, he ought to be."

A chest of coins would be worth a good deal if it were filled only with copper. If it were silver, it would buy a longship and pay for the men in it. The vessels and horns would make the prize richer, and in an English earl's hall there were always good weapons, fine cloth, and slaves worth selling.

There was also Rosamund. Why she was in his thoughts, Haakon didn't know. Maybe he had been too long without a woman. But for some unexplained reason, he didn't feel easy in his mind about her marrying this drunken Harud. She sounded worthy of a better man. If they could raid the castle and carry her off—

Of course. I'll give her to Bjorn. He needs someone like her—strong and sensible and not so beautiful he'll have to fight other men for her.

Haakon laughed to himself at the thought of Bjorn with a woman of his own, but the strange unease in his mind didn't go away. If he had to describe it, he would have said it felt as if he were wearing a helmet just slightly too tight.

"Very well," he said. "Do you know a way to reach the castle that lets us get back to the ships if Edmund and his men have returned?"

"I do."

"Then you'll have your vengeance and also a helmsman's share of whatever we carry off. Perhaps we can teach Edmund Oswainsson—"

He broke off, for Gunnar knelt before him now, gripping his knees like a drowning man clinging to a log and obviously trying not to weep. Haakon seized the poet by both shoulders and pulled him to his feet.

"You've done enough kneeling for one free man's life, Gunnar. Stand up, and if you want to do me a favor, go to the armorer and ask him for a file." Gunnar was still fighting back tears as he hurried off.

The thought of this Rosamund returned as Gunnar disappeared. With it came some of the words Haakon remembered hearing from what might have been Thor last night:

You will know our wishes when they come to you. Do not fear that we will ever leave you groping in the darkness.

Haakon laughed, almost bitterly. Even if Rosamund's fate was a matter of concern to the gods, and preventing her marriage to Harud Olafsson was the first service he would do them, that would not keep him from groping in darkness. He would be groping until he knew how much of that dream-fraught night was part of this world, and how much was simply a dream. The ax—it felt so light, so fine in his fist. The ax, at least, was real.

Haakon sat down on a rock and laid the golden ax across his knees. God work or man work, an ax was an ax, and mysteries were no reason to neglect a good weapon. He would file it sharp—sharp enough to cut through the men of Edmund's castle.

V

In four days both ships were fit for sea once more. Most of the labor went into *Wave Walker*, but there were also repairs on *Red Hawk*, now that there was spare time and extra hands to make them. Snorri, the carpenter, said that he'd take better care of a ship like *Wave Walker* than of a woman.

"No matter how good you are to her, a woman can always turn against you," said the carpenter. "If you give a ship everything she needs, even the sea itself cannot turn her against you. She is yours in life and death, asking only for care and a good wind!"

From time to time Haakon lent a hand on the ships, where his strength and endurance could be useful for the rougher work. The rest of his time was spent getting to know *Wave Walker*'s men: the possible leaders, the known cowards, the best swordsmen, the ones most likely to stumble over their own feet before the fighting even started. However, there were few real weaklings left after the last battle.

All seemed willing to take orders from Knut One-Eye, and most seemed willing to follow Gunnar Thorsten. So Haakon had both Knut and Gunnar swear oaths to serve him as lesser chiefs, and then all the men of both ships swore to obey these new leaders as they would Haakon and Bjorn. Some of *Red Hawk*'s men grumbled, but all of them took the oaths. Haakon was glad. Knut and Gunnar were too worthy to be used only as swords in a fight.

Two wounded men died the day before they set sail, one man from each ship. There was nothing to sacrifice and barely enough wood for a proper pyre, but Haakon promised the ghosts of the two men everything they could ask the moment he could give it. He had them buried on the beach. Farther inland the barrow might be safer from storms and robbers, but he wasn't going to bury any honest man inland on this island of mysteries.

All during these days and even as they sailed south into the Irish Sea, thoughts of Rosamund and the marriage she was about to make kept creeping into Haakon's mind. He did not let those thoughts turn him from his main work: planning the coming raid and teaching each of the men his part in that battle.

Clouds blacked out what would have been the last glow of sunset. They looked swollen, ominous, ready to rain at any moment. As he led his men through the English woods, Haakon thought to himself that he would have been happier without the threat of rain. Only Gunnar knew this countryside well, and Haakon worried that they might not find the castle before being discovered.

More black-gray sky became apparent through the tree-tops as the woods thinned out ahead. Haakon slowed his pace. He didn't want to burst out on the bare hillside into the view of any riders who might be on the road at the bottom of the valley. They could warn not only Edmund's Hold but the whole countryside.

The earl's castle stood on the western tip of the steep-

sided cape called the Ram's Head overlooking the shore
for half a day's march north and south. Half the year it
held a strong force of the earl's fighting men, ready to
move against any attackers. The other half of the year they
were scattered to their homes or far away with their lord
in King Alfred's service.

The cliffs of the Ram's Head protected the castle against
attack from the sea. Inland, rugged hills left only a narrow
valley with a road running through it as an approach. For
extra protection, the earl had a walled farm defending the
road at the narrowest point of the valley.

Gunnar Thorsten knew all the weaknesses of both the
castle and the farm. He had made his desperate escape
through the hills and had seen several paths where men
on foot could reach the farm undetected. On Gunnar's
knowledge Haakon had laid his plans.

Twenty men, under Snorri Longfoot, would be left
behind to guard the beached ships, then would bring the
vessels around the cape to the castle—or if the worst
happened, try to get them home. Twenty-five men, led by
Bjorn and guided by Gunnar, would slip through the hills
and surprise the farm from the west.

A dozen men, under Haakon, would cross the hills a
little to the east of the farm and show themselves in front
of it. They would draw the defenders' attention while
Bjorn crept close and would also watch for anyone coming
up the road.

If the castle was strongly held, the Norsemen would
loot the farm, then return through the woods to their ship.
If the castle was lightly held, they'd try taking it as well.
That would be a more dangerous battle, but with Gunnar's

knowledge, Haakon felt his men would have a fair chance once they'd reached the castle walls.

Snorri had two keen-sighted men perched in a tall tree near the ships' hiding place in a secluded cove. There he could see them, and they could relay any signals from the men attacking the castle. Then the victors would climb down the cliffs with their booty. The cliffs of the Ram's Head protected the castle against attackers climbing up from below, but were no real barriers to men climbing down.

The castle should yield enough booty to let Haakon be generous with all the men of both ships and pay for repairing *Wave Walker* as well. Even if they only took the farm, there would be weapons and goods to carry off, and the memory of a successful fight side-by-side would help bind the two crews more firmly together.

Haakon saw open ground ahead, and beyond, dim hillsides. They were almost at the rim of the valley, and he turned to tell Knut to halt the men following them. A blast of wind swept up from the valley as he did, and his voice was lost in the moan of swaying trees. As the wind died away he and his men heard voices and the lowing of oxen from down in the valley.

Knut had the other men concealed in the brush even before Haakon was able to creep forward to where he could look down into the valley. Then, on hands and knees, Knut joined his chief.

Below them a flickering lantern showed a group of men and four heavily laden oxcarts at the bottom of the valley less than two hundred paces away.

The men were gathered around the lead cart, apparently fixing a wheel. Haakon counted no more than ten or twelve men, four of them with spears and shields.

The carts might not be worth much as booty, unless they held something easily carried away. But it wouldn't be safe to leave this party behind, possibly to give warning, and the carts might prove useful. If Haakon's men could disguise themselves as friends that the defenders expected, surprise would come more easily.

"Bring the others up," he told Knut.

As Haakon's men joined him, he could see the Englishmen stepping back from the crippled cart, their work apparently finished. While the drivers were climbing up into their seats again, Haakon gave his orders. The carts were just starting to move when Haakon rose to his feet, his archers beside him.

It was long range for archery in this feeble light, and Haakon wished he hadn't sent Hagar the Simple with Bjorn. The archers still did well enough. One armed man went down from the first two arrows. The others whirled about, trying to identify the danger or from where it was coming. But it was too late. As a second guard collapsed, an arrow in his thigh, Knut and four men with spears reached throwing range.

The spears picked off a third guard and two of the drivers. The last guard caught a spear in his shield and threw his own. Knut watched the spear, bobbed his head just enough to let it go over him, drew his sword as he straightened up, and closed with the man. The archers slung their bows and drew knives, then joined the fight around the carts. Just behind the archers Haakon charged in with the rest of the men.

When his feet hit the bare earth of the road, Haakon

dropped his shield, sheathed his sword, and unslung the ax from his back. There was plenty of room for fighting, only a few opponents, and none of them archers. This was as good a chance as any to test the golden ax in battle.

When he unslung the ax, Haakon noticed that its head was glowing with a pale, blurred, golden aura. If it wasn't glowing, Haakon's eyes were playing strange jokes on him. No. He was sure the ax had a light of its own.

The moments Haakon took changing his weapons were nearly his last. Two Englishmen who had been hiding under the bellies of the lead cart's oxen now saw only one man standing between them and safety. They leaped out and dashed for the far side of the road.

Haakon moved across the path of the second man, who slipped and fell. Desperately he struck up at Haakon with a long knife and would have castrated him if Haakon's mail hadn't reached below his groin. Haakon brought the ax down hard on the man's chest and left him dying in the road while he chased the other.

The Englishman had a good lead and wore no armor, but Haakon was as determined to catch the man as the man was to get away. Haakon caught the man halfway up the hillside and swung at his back. The blow knocked the man down. He rolled practically under Haakon's feet, gasping and sobbing, half-mad with fear. Haakon struck him in the belly, and a stench rose as the man fouled himself. Haakon raised the ax for a third blow, but it wasn't needed.

The Englishman was crying like a baby with the pain of his wounds, but his wide eyes were blank. Haakon shifted the ax to one hand, drew his dagger, and slit the dying man's throat. As he fell silent, Haakon wiped the ax on the

Englishman's clothing, then rested it on his shoulder. The
Englishman would tell no living person what he'd seen,
and the other men down on the road would have been too
far away to notice the ax's glow.

When Haakon rejoined his men, the fighting was over.
All the Englishmen were dead, although Knut was having
the carts searched to make sure. None of the Norse was
hurt beyond the ability to march or fight. Knut had also
learned valuable information from two of the dying men.

"The earl himself's a good ways off," he told Haakon.
"The two older sons are with him, and most of the men.
The youngest son's visiting Harud Olafsson in Ireland and
has some men with him. They might be back later tonight,
but again they might not. The carts were bringing up ale
and meat in preparation for the betrothal feast planned for
next week. Edmund, Harud, and all the men are expected
to return soon in readiness for the festivities."

So the castle was weakly held, at least for a few hours
more. Haakon considered for a moment the tempting idea
of using the disguise provided by the carts to march
straight up to the castle to surprise it. He decided to hold
fast to his original plan of going first to the farm. Moving
on the castle without dealing with the farm risked getting
his men caught with enemies to their front and rear, with
no hope of retreat and danger of total disaster.

"You've done good work, Knut. Now we strip the
Englishmen. Some of us should pull on their clothes and
hide our weapons in the straw in the bottom of the carts."

"We'll be able to move faster if we lighten the carts,"
said Knut.

"I agree, but let's throw out the meat first. I'm not

hungry, but I know I'm going to be thirsty after this night's work, so keep the ale."

That roused a laugh, and the men started peeling the shoes and breeches off the English. Haakon scrambled up into one of the carts and pushed barrels of salt meat out the back. As they fell, Knut rolled them to one side of the road.

Their visit to Earl Edmund was well begun, Haakon decided—although the strange light from the head of the golden ax was a new mystery. There was no question that it glowed, and yet none of his men had mentioned it. Had they been too involved with their own struggles to have noticed? Had they forgotten by the battle's end? Or was it possible the aura was visible only to him?

Bjorn clung to his perch as the wind rose. He was glad he hadn't climbed further up the tree. The branch under him was as thick as a man's thigh and yet was bucking under him like a half-broken horse.

Fortunately he could see enough from where he was. The farm must have once been a wealthy freeholder's. Now a wall of sharpened logs driven into a bank of earth surrounded a house, two huts, a barn, and a well. No outlaws or escaping slaves could hope to menace it. Forty determined Norsemen were another matter.

A fire burned in a stone-lined pit in the center of the farm, and a faint glow crept out around the wooden shutters of the main house. The light showed two men tending the fire, three more at the gate, and a sixth pulling up his breeches as he walked from behind the barn. None of them looked hurried, suspicious, or frightened. *They probably think this wind's enough to make the whole coast safe against ships landing.*

The man who'd been relieving himself behind the barn went into the house. He had to struggle to keep the wind from snatching the door out of his hands. As he finally closed the door behind him, one of the guards at the gate raised his spear and waved it. This brought the other two guards up to him. One cupped his hands around his mouth, shouting to someone on the road, invisible in the darkness to the east.

Bjorn saw Gunnar step out from his hiding place and raise both hands over his head—their signal asking permission to attack. Bjorn gripped the branch with both thighs and one hand and stuck the other hand straight out in front of him—their signal for "No."

Gunnar's eager, and I don't blame him. But I'm not going to let anyone move a step until we see who's coming to visit. Then the visitors took solid shape out of the night. Four oxcarts, their drivers sitting huddled and cloaked against the wind, and spearmen marching beside them. *Haakon must have let them go by, rather than risk warning the men at the farm by attacking them.*

Two guards climbed on top of the gate and shouted down inside the walls. The doors of the main house and one of the huts opened; men trickled out, some unarmed or half-dressed. The drivers climbed down from their perches and clustered around the oxen of the lead cart. One of the spearmen, a thickset man in a hooded cloak, went to the middle cart and began searching in the straw around the barrels.

Then events shifted so quickly that ever afterward they ran together in Bjorn's memory. A horseman came trotting up from the direction of the castle, slowing to a walk as he approached the farm.

The spearman pulled a long cloth-wrapped bundle out of the straw, tore the cloth away, raised a two-handed Norse ax over his head, and swung it back and forth three times. The carters surrounded a guard near the farm's entrance and suddenly drew their knives and swords. The unfortunate Englishman vanished before he could scream.

Bjorn could hear the battle cry, "*Haakon! Haakon! Haakon!*"

The horseman was close enough to see the guard's death and hear the war cries. He jerked his horse around so violently that it panicked, squealed, and reared, just short of throwing him off.

Gunnar Thorsten also must have heard the war cries. Without waiting for word or signal from Bjorn, he burst into the open and plunged down the hillside toward the farm. As he ran, he shouted with all the breath he could spare from running—no poetry, but obscene descriptions of the ancestors and habits of Earl Edmund and all the men who served him.

After Gunnar, all the other men of Bjorn's party came howling and waving weapons. Some of them weren't as surefooted as Gunnar, but even the ones who slipped and fell bounced back up again.

Two dozen Norsemen bursting out of the night was too much for the horse. It reared one more time, put its head down, and bolted toward the castle. Hagar the Simple stopped, nocked an arrow to the bow he was carrying strung in one hand, and shot. But even Hagar couldn't bring down a target vanishing into the darkness at a full gallop.

Outside the gate, Haakon's men pulled one of the carts against the wall to use as a step for climbing over the palisade. Inside, more English reinforcements poured out of the house and the hut. It looked as if the raiders were going to be fighting against a force with at least their own numbers, and there might be more coming down on them the moment the castle was warned. At least the earl and his men weren't at home—Haakon's signal with the ax— waving it three times—meant he'd learned that much.

Bjorn jumped to the ground, landing hard but on soft earth, snatched up his shield, drew his sword, and ran down the hill to the farm.

"I will not assist with the selection! I do not care! Better still, get me lengths of black. I will wear black when I marry Harud," Rosamund said, wrenching material out of Guthrun's arms and depositing the yards onto the floor.

Guthrun gathered the cloth bolts and hurried out of the room. She had served Rosamund long enough to know to avoid these storms. *Poor lady,* she thought, *going from a devil of a father to a devil of a husband.*

Rosamund sank onto her bed, sighed, and cast off the fur coverings. She would have no sleep tonight, and for a moment she almost hated Wulf for being able to sleep so soundly, untroubled by the ways of this world. The big Irish wolfhound lay in his usual place at the foot of the bed, only an occasional twitch of his ears showing that he was alive.

She was not surprised by her tension. She'd been at work since before dawn these past three days, making sure all was clean and orderly for her father, her brothers, and their men. The fruits of her labors wouldn't last long after their return. With a hundred fighting men inside the walls, how could it? But she was determined to display her ability to manage the castle, even if she half killed both herself and the servants. That wasn't the only reason, Rosamund admitted. While she was readying the castle, she had little time to think about her betrothal.

She had met Harud Olafsson only once, when he and his father, Olaf Haraldsson, came to Ram's Head to negotiate the terms of the marriage and the size of the dowry. She found father and son equally repugnant. The thought of moving ato their steading in Ireland sent convulsions of nausea through her system. Then she had overheard some of the servants talking. In their contact with the visitors' attendants, they had learned of the fates of Olafsson's first two wives: One had been sorely used by her father-in-law until her mysterious demise. The other had been beaten to death.

Now her revulsion was mixed with fear, producing a state akin to desperation. She was willing to sink to treachery herself, if need be, to escape this marriage and to save her life.

Above the snores of the maids on their pallets along the walls, she could hear the moan of the wind outside. It must have risen while she sat thinking, between waking and sleeping. Some of it was finding a way through chinks in the walls and blowing cold on her bare skin. She shivered, clasping her arms around her breasts, then reached out of bed to pick up her shift.

She'd just pulled it over her head when wild shouts from outside drowned out both the wind and the maids' snores.

"Norse! Norse! Norse at the farm!"

Rosamund sprang out of bed to wake the maids. Wulf was at her side.

The first two maids she roused heard the cries of "Norse!" and their screams woke the rest. Rosamund struggled to hide the fact that her own voice wasn't entirely steady. Norse attacking the farm that guarded the landward approaches to the castle meant the lives of everyone here were threatened.

By the time the women were quiet, Rosamund could hear the uproar of men running about and arming. Someone was shouting, "Lady Rosamund! Be you awake?" and was pounding on the chamber door. She threw a cloak on over her shift, unbarred the door, and stepped out to meet Aelfric. He was the oldest of her father's thanes and chief over the fighting men left behind to protect the castle.

He was nearly sixty, but the prospect of a fight made him look twenty years younger. "Norse at the farm, lady! A shipload, maybe more. Came out of the forest."

Rosamund had learned a good deal about warfare from listening to the men of her family. Norse coming out of the forest might have cut off the farm, and a shipload might be enough to take it.

"We be holding here, lady," Aelfric went on. "Can't go down there with so few men here."

That was a harsh but undeniable truth. There were no more than twenty-five or thirty fighting men left in the castle, and perhaps as many more men and boys among the servants who knew one end of a spear from the other. Everyone would be needed to hold the castle; not one could be spared for a march through the darkness to the farm along a narrow road where the Norse might already be lying in wait.

Between Wulf's barking and the whimpers of the maids, it took Rosamund a moment to realize that Aelfric was asking her a question, not handing down his own decision.

"Hold t'outer walls, or just the mound?" Aelfric asked again.

She silenced Wulf and the maids and sorted out her thoughts. Edmund's Hold was divided into two parts: An outer wall of heavy logs, with a ditch at its exterior base, ran across the neck of the peninsula that ended in the Ram's Head; behind this outer wall was a level space with stables, storehouses, the smithy, the brewery, the bakery, and lodgings for most of the fighting men.

On a rise to the west of this lay the great hall with the sleeping chambers for the earl's household as well as more storehouses for food, drink, and weapons. The hall was surrounded by another wooden wall, higher than the outer wall, but there was no ditch. The soil at the end of the peninsula was too rocky for easy digging.

The great hall could stand off attackers by itself well enough. Should they abandon the outer wall and concentrate the defenders inside the defenses of the great hall? She had to decide instantly.

"Hold the outer wall! If we let go, the Norsemen will surely burn and loot everything up to the wall of the great hall. That's too much to lose to a handful of Norse. Fight them for every foot of Edmund's Hold!"

Aelfric smiled broadly. "Aye. Could be just a handful of Norse, too. Lads at the farm—they may do some good work and cull out a few."

The young men at the farm might die under Viking weapons, but before they did they'd probably kill a number of the enemy. There might be no more than thirty or forty Norse coming up to the outer wall, and against that many even the slim force of defenders could hold out until help arrived. She ordered Aelfric to send messengers for aid.

"God be with you!" she said.

"And with you!"

He bowed, then hurried down the stairs to the great hall below. Rosamund found the women staring at her, waiting to be told what to do next.

A sudden glow half lit the hall as Aelfric went out, and she smelled wood smoke. Her men must have lit the beacon fire to call to the castle's aid any English ships or men in sight. She fought down a desire to scramble up the ladder to the roof of the hall and watch the castle's defenders preparing themselves.

"Birgitta, Edwina, go down and fill all the buckets you can find. Elfrida, bring up a sack of bread. Guthrun, go to the storeroom and bring back—" she counted the women around her "—seven spears. You all have knives?"

The women nodded, apparently not frightened by the implications of what Rosamund was saying but more likely not fully understanding them.

Below in the hall, the glow died away as someone pulled shut the door and began piling furniture in front of it. Outside, the voices were also dying away, but Rosamund heard the iron clang of the alarm gong—as if anyone in the castle still needed warning.

Bjorn caught up with his men at the farm just as the heads of the first defenders appeared over the wall. With four arrows, Thorkell removed three defenders.

Meanwhile, the four strongest Vikings squatted down in

pairs, shields on their backs to make steps for scaling the wall. Bjorn leaped up on one step, and Turo the Finn from *Wave Walker* climbed up on the other. An English face glared into Bjorn's. He smashed his shield into it. The man screamed and staggered sideways until his screams ended under Turo's ax. Bjorn and Black Ayolf heaved themselves over the palisade and onto the platform running around the inside perimeter of the wall. Hagar the Simple climbed quickly up onto the shields after Turo, while shooting down into the farm. The shield-bearers swayed under the archer, but Hagar could have shot accurately even if he were hanging by his feet from the branch of a tree.

Bjorn's men spread out along the platform after they climbed up the shield steps, the archers first and the men with spears and swords after them. Hagar held his next shot, shouting to the other bowmen to do the same. Then the door to the main house opened and out spilled Englishmen, some carrying torches. Thorkell shot one of the torchbearers, and Bjorn shouted to his spearmen still on the ground to join Haakon in attacking the gate. Bjorn jumped down to the ground inside the wall, and the Vikings with him followed, screaming, eager to come to grips with the defenders.

Bjorn's archers fired at the door of the house to keep the Englishmen inside so that his men actually outnumbered the opponents in the courtyard. The Englishmen finally broke through the fire and out the door and streamed toward the gate, opening it to flee—but they met Haakon's men coming in. The sweeps of Haakon's ax cleared Englishmen from his path as if they were wheat under the scythe.

Caught between two bands of Norsemen with no way of escape, some of the Englishmen threw down their weapons and cried for mercy. Haakon rested the bloody axhead on the ground and shouted loud his orders:

"Hold off there! Hold off! They're giving up! Take their weapons and tie their hands!"

Several more Englishmen died before the fighting stopped. Others refused to yield until Haakon threatened to strike them down where they stood. The rest were swiftly made prisoner, and Haakon turned his thoughts to his next move.

With Gunnar's knowledge of the castle, he'd been able to make his plans for attacking it long since. The only decision still to be made was whether he should attack it at all. There was just one dead Norseman, and only four of the wounded couldn't fight. On the other hand, there were many more prisoners than he'd expected, at least thirty. Most were young farmhands, but the rear guard left at the farm would still have to watch them, as well as watch for the arrival of more English.

Forward, he decided. Marching against even the most weakly defended castle with fewer than thirty fighting men wasn't going to be easy. His advantage was that he knew the castle's weakness. Going forward with good men who'd already won two solid victories tonight promised a rich reward.

Haakon counted off six fit men and the four wounded to hold the farm and guard the prisoners. "If more English come, set the farm on fire and come to us. Otherwise, wait until I send word from the castle."

As his men checked his prisoners' bindings and their own weapons, Haakon cleaned his ax. The head and handle were caked with blood, and Haakon found this otherwise ugly sight a relief. He'd heard tales of magical weapons that actually drank the blood of the men they slew and grew stronger with each slaying until they were the very masters of the men who wielded them. If he'd thought the golden ax could be one of these weapons, he'd have dropped it off the nearest cliff into the sea.

He was pulling up a handful of damp grass to wipe off the ax when Bjorn joined him. "It served you well, Haakon."

Haakon nodded absently, tossing aside the soiled grass. He paused for a moment, considering. Then he turned to Bjorn. "Did you notice anything about this ax? Anything . . . out of the ordinary, I mean."

Bjorn narrowed his eyes, then shook his head. "What do you mean? A curse?"

"No, Bjorn, not a curse. A light. Have you seen a light?"

"From the torches, you mean. A reflection, Haakon? There is nothing unusual about a torch casting a reflection on metal."

"The glow is not from the torches, Bjorn. It is from within the ax," Haakon softly replied.

Bjorn stared, amazed. But he said nothing.

"I'll be happier not to hear you talking about it," Haakon said. "At least not until we've finished tonight's battle."

"You'll trust the ax?" Bjorn seemed worried about any danger that might come to Haakon from the golden ax.

Haakon started wiping the ax blade. "I've trusted it twice tonight, and I'm still alive."

VI

Everything possible had been done by Rosamund. The women, children, and old men were crammed into the private chambers like salt herring into a barrel. Below, the door to the great hall was barricaded by piled benches and chests and defended by a handful of servants with spears. They could not fight with warriors' strength or ability, but if the Norse reached the hall weary, battered, and thinned in numbers, the servants might provide adequate defenses. If not . . . Rosamund refused to dwell on such painful questions.

The crowded chamber's darkness was hardly broken by the yellow light from rush dips. It stank of sweat and fear. Rosamund shook off the imploring hands clutching at her skirts and darted to the foot of the ladder leading up to the roof.

Wulf followed her, then barked when he saw where she was going. He could leap at the throat of a full-grown stag and bring it down, but he wasn't nimble enough to follow his mistress, or the castle's cats, up ladders. She scratched his head.

"No, Wulf. You stay here." Wulf made a rumbling sound in his throat and lay down with his head on his paws. Right now he looked harmless, but one should not be fooled by

appearances, unless willing to suffer painful or even deadly consequences.

Rosamund scrambled up the ladder with speed and
agility. On the roof, the wind nearly blew the cloak from
her shoulders, but it also blew away much of the fear
tearing at her. Whatever might happen tonight, she could
face it better in the clean air, under God's sky, able to see
the enemy.

A castle spearman approached. "Lady, this is no place—"

"This is my place, and I'll stay here."

The spearman swallowed and looked at his feet. He was
one of the village boys to whom her father was giving their
first training in arms this summer. He was perhaps younger
than she and likely not to see another sunrise if the Norse
forced their way inside the walls.

One of the stewards joined them, holding his spear
gingerly. "Lady Rosamund, your father'll flay our backs
open to the bone if anything happens to you."

She saw a shield lying on the planks.

"Give me that. It should be enough against arrows."

Neither the man nor the boy liked it, but the only
alternative was getting her off the roof by laying hands on
her. That, no lowborn knave would dare. They'd just
finished tightening her shield's straps when the alarm
gong began sounding again. Rosamund looked out beyond
the wall and saw a solid block of armored men marching
out of the forest.

Pride kept her from kneeling, but not from whispering
an urgent prayer. "Lord Jesus, give me the strength to
withstand this assault. If I face my death, help me meet it
courageously. Help me find the path to safety for my
people and myself."

*   *   *

The English defenders were silent as Haakon's men
halted just out of bowshot range of the outer wall of the
castle. His face cloaked against recognition, Gunnar stalked
back and forth like a hunting dog trying to pick up a scent.
He was studying the wall. It was difficult to count logs in
the darkness, but after a moment Gunnar turned to Haakon
and pointed.

"There—the seven logs starting with the thirtieth one to
the left of the gate."

"You're certain?"

Gunnar's smile was that of a hungry wolf. "I've heard
the earl cursing that spot often enough. It's weak—no
depth to the logs."

Each man with Haakon knew what to do. There'd been
no arguments about places of honor after the men realized
that there would be danger enough to go around. Right
now, Haakon's men were a single weapon, like the golden
ax itself. Haakon surveyed the wall and the flickering
torches on top of it, then the men around him. The ax
handle began to radiate warmth into Haakon's arms and
shoulders, and the head emanated a subtle aura.

"Time to start our work."

Bjorn and Gunnar led ten men forward. They held ax
and mattock, and each man also carried an extra shield.
Arrows came at them from the wall, but the shooting was
both slow and poor. The extra shields brought them safely
to the wall and down into the ditch at its base. There they
were safe from arrows, except for those shot along the wall
at an angle, and these were infrequent. Under the protec-

tion of shield-bearers, the men with the axes and mattocks went to work.

Some logs of the wall had struck solid rock before being driven in all the way. From the outside they looked no different, because at the top they'd been cut off at the same level. In the ditch, however, a handful of men digging hard could quickly strip away enough earth so that the logs could be exposed and pulled out with ropes.

Except for Haakon and Hagar's archers, the other Norsemen were crouched behind oxcarts hauled up as shelter from arrows. The archers climbed up on top of the carts, piled their arrows ready to hand, and went to work eliminating the Englishmen along the wall. Torches on the ramparts made the Englishmen who'd set them alight easy to see without showing up the attackers. After a while the Englishmen realized this and the torches that hadn't been knocked down by falling bodies were snuffed out. Now the Norse in the ditch at work undermining the wall were practically invisible to their enemies.

Haakon's archers went on shooting. They'd captured enough English arrows at the farm to keep the wall's defenders busy and still have enough of their own arrows for the rest of the fighting.

Bjorn materialized out of the darkness and crouched next to Haakon. "The wall is coming down, just as Gunnar promised. For a time I was afraid we were being led into a trap."

"I can't understand why the castle's defenders aren't pouring out at us yet. Either their forces are terribly weak or—"

"—Or they're letting us tire ourselves. They might not be so weak when the close fighting begins."

Haakon nodded. The torches were all extinguished, and English arrows came only rarely. Then they stopped entirely, and Haakon wondered why. The defenders were strangely silent, and the only sounds to be heard were Gunnar's men digging up the wall's logs and Bjorn's heavy breathing. *What were the English doing? What did their silence mean?* Haakon wondered.

Suddenly, there was a wrenching crash, and the sound of twisting, squealing timbers rent the silence. From the ditch where Gunnar's men were working came a savage shout of triumph.

"The wall!" Bjorn shouted. "It's open!"

Sure enough, Haakon could see the breach where the timbers of the palisade had been ripped free, exposing an entry to the defensive works. The English must have heard their enemy undermining the wall. They had feared this was coming, Haakon realized, and he called his men to attack. The English were silent because they were fleeing from the outer wall. Perhaps at this very moment they were running like rabbits through the open yard between the outer wall and the great hall. This was the moment to seize! This was the moment of victory!

The Vikings battered their way through the gaping hole, striking down the few brave but outnumbered defenders who tried to slow them. Haakon charged to the front of his men and threw himself into the fury of battle. In that instant, he saw that, indeed, Englishmen were trapped by the Viking breakthrough. They were struggling to mass their defense, but there were not enough of them to beat off the attackers.

Luck was with Haakon tonight—luck and the golden ax. In its light was the promise of Viking victory and of the great booty that only the mightiest warriors dared dream of.

Rosamund looked down from the roof as the Vikings and Aelfric's men clashed. Peering through the battlement, she managed to single out Aelfric fending off two Norsemen and heard him curse the attackers hoarsely. Then, as he tried to maneuver his back to a wall, he was struck in the side, and a sharp cry escaped Rosamund's lips. Aelfric collapsed on the ground, lifeless. The men had no leader now. Rosamund's heart thundered with fear, and she had little hope for victory.

She closed her eyes and listened to the battle's terrible sounds: metal beating on metal, shields cracking, and men cursing with anger or screaming with pain. The fight lurched backward toward the great hall itself and into the glow from the dying beacon fire. The Norse attacked in a solid mass of men, blood dripping from their weapons and armor. The English backed up, stubborn but without hope. Her cry at Aelfric's death had alerted the attackers to her presence on the roof, but Rosamund could not force herself to take refuge.

Rosamund found a lump of iron fixed in her throat as she tried to swallow. They'd lost the fight. How much else would they lose?

Everything, said a harsh voice in her mind.

No! Not if I can do anything. But what?

For a moment, Rosamund was tempted to stay on the roof, hidden. After the battle was over and the booty carted away, perhaps she would have enough time to escape her father and Harud Olafsson. They would think she'd been kidnapped or ransomed. She could go to a

convent, perhaps. No, she couldn't do any of that. It was
her duty to remain with her people and share whatever
fate came to them. Perhaps she would be able to save
them and herself.

She'd have to face whatever came next down below, in
the great hall. The thought made her stomach twist for a
moment, but accepting the fate of the vanquished inevita-
bly followed on the heels of the defeat. Only in the hall
could she speak to both Norse and to her own people in
time to do any good.

And these *were* her people. Anything she could do for
them, she had to do. She had an idea. It was wild and
reckless. But if the Viking leader could control his men,
and if he wanted what most men wanted... Perhaps her
plan might work.

She felt at the dagger in her belt. Yes, it might be a plan
for saving her people and her father's holding. She turned
to descend the ladder, knowing that if her plan failed, she
would die.

VII

Rosamund, with the shield on her arm, came down the
stairs to the great hall. Wulf was close at her heels.

The servants stared numbly from behind chests and
from under tables and benches as she walked toward the
door. Viking fists and weapons pounded on the outside—a
pounding that echoed around the room like thunder.

She pointed at the nearest man. "Get up and unbar the door. If we can't hold, we'd better talk."

"With them?" he said, half-choking.

"Yes."

"My lady, have you gone mad?" The man scrambled to his feet and came toward her. She stepped back and drew her dagger. Wulf bared his teeth and growled.

"Open this door!" roared a voice from outside. It was a voice that made her think of storm waves on a rocky coast. "Open, or be burned out!" His Norse tongue was close enough to her own Saxon so she had no trouble understanding him. Neither did the others in the hall.

Rosamund looked around her. "You heard him!" She pointed her dagger at the man who had called her mad. "You! Hold your tongue!" Two other men lifted the bar on the door and pulled heavy wooden chests away from it. Then they sprang aside as if Hel itself were opening in front of the door. In the hall, Rosamund and Wulf were standing together when the Norse entered.

Three of them came in at once. All were tall, all wore blood-stained armor, and all had faces like Death's mercenaries come to scour life from the earth. Rosamund saw that the man on the right had only one eye, and that the face of the man on the left was hidden in the hood of his cloak.

She saw the man in the middle more clearly. He was darker than the others, hair and beard brown rather than fair like most Norse. He looked shorter, but this was only because he was so much broader across the chest and shoulders. He wore a whole armory by himself—a shield on one arm, a broken-off spear in the other hand, a sheathed sword on his belt, and an ax slung across his back. He stepped forward, Rosamund backed away, and Wulf gave the growl she knew meant he was ready to leap.

Haakon's spear point whipped around like a striking adder, and his arm curved, ready to throw. "Call off your dog, lady," he said softly. "Call him off, or I'll kill him."

Rosamund gripped Wulf's collar. "Down, Wulf! Down! Friend!" She had never seen three more fear-inspiring faces in her life and could only hope Wulf would believe what she told him rather than what he sensed.

Reluctantly, Wulf obeyed, letting himself be dragged backward as more Norse followed the first three into the hall. Most of them looked more savage than the three chiefs, but Rosamund found their presence almost a relief. With only three Norse in the hall, some wild fool among her people might be tempted into a desperate attack and bring down ruin on all of them. With twenty armed Norse in the hall, her men's moves would be more predictable.

The cloaked man's hood slipped down, and the chunk of iron returned to Rosamund's throat as she recognized Gunnar Thorsten. She'd never cursed him while he was a slave in the castle, but now she would have cheerfully seen him sinking slowly into a pit of red-hot coals. It was probably at his urging that these Norse had come to cause her people's destruction.

The Viking chief who had threatened Wulf was now standing a little ahead of his two companions, staring at her in a way that would have made her blush under other circumstances. Her heart pounded in her throat, and she felt an inexplicable force within her, drawing her toward him. There was something in his voice, perhaps, or his eyes. Or perhaps she was being drawn to her death.

The hall was silent as the Norse realized they weren't going to be turned loose at once.

When Haakon saw the slender blond young woman standing in his path, his first thought was: *The maiden from the battlement! If this is the lady Rosamund, then Gunnar may be a good poet, but he's no judge of women.*

Her face was a little too long and her mouth definitely too wide. Also, the tangled hair, the cloak hanging like dead leaves from a tree in autumn, and the complexion as pale as wheat flour didn't help. In spite of all this, she was still the most striking woman he'd ever seen, even though she was now standing like a statue carved from ice.

She stands like a warrior defending a bridge, sworn to hold it or die, he thought. *I'll give that kind of courage the honor it deserves.*

Rosamund spoke first. "This is Edmund's Hold, and I am the lady Rosamund, daughter to Earl Edmund."

"I am Haakon Olesson," he replied. "Here you have Knut Aleksson. I think you already know Gunnar Thorsten."

"You are the leader of these men, Haakon Olesson." She swallowed, then her face was a mask again. "I desire to speak with you privately."

Haakon smiled, and they moved to a corner of the great hall, where she turned to face the huge Viking.

"You have won only part of your victory tonight, Haakon Olesson. It will be easier to have the rest if you don't need to fight for it. I will pledge no interference from my people in your removal of booty. You've got good men here, but not too many of them. How much can you win if we decide we'd rather die than be taken quietly? And if you do win, will there be enough of you left to get away from here? My father and . . . his men are expected at any time."

"You interest me, Lady Rosamund. What do you expect to gain from this?"

"You must swear not to burn or rape or destroy the hold. You must pledge that your men will have only those women who consent." Rosamund smiled, although it was the sort of smile one expected to see on the face of a skull.

Haakon stood, considering. He looked back at his men who stood tensed, waiting to kill. Knut was flexing his hands by his side, obviously restraining himself by a slender margin.

"No. I do not accept your offer. My men would fight all night. Fatigue is a complaint of women, not of Vikings." He turned toward his men.

"Wait!" Rosamund hissed. "There is more. There is a great treasure hidden in the castle. My dowry—three chests of coin. One is gold, two are silver. That will buy you many ships and men, Haakon."

Haakon turned and looked at her. That would be enough for ten attacks on Olaf Haraldsson. "Go on. Where is the treasure?"

"Oh, no, Haakon. That is part of the deal you and I must make. I cannot tell you where it is until I have your oath that no harm will come to my people or the castle."

The great hall was silent, awaiting Haakon's response. He looked over toward his men. Their eyes had narrowed at the mention of gold and silver. This was the treasure of which Gunnar spoke. She was not bluffing.

"Gunnar! Do you know where it is hidden?"

"No, Haakon, I do not."

Hagar the Simple snarled, "You give me a few minutes

with her, and she will be telling us everything you want to know."

"If you take a step, I will kill myself," Rosamund said, pulling her dagger from her cloak and holding it firmly beneath her ribs. "Then you will have no treasure. Go on, burn down the castle if you wish; you will never find the treasure. I will die, my people will die, and you will leave here with nothing."

Haakon looked at Gunnar. "She will do it, Haakon. I know her."

Haakon moved to his men to consider this. Bjorn spoke for them. "That gold would make for a large force of many followers. I would be willing to swear an oath to get the treasure."

"As would I."

"And I, too."

The others nodded in assent and relaxed in their posture. Haakon moved back to Rosamund. "I will swear that no one will be killed and that your castle will not be destroyed if you show me the treasure."

This time Rosamund looked to Gunnar for verification. "Can Haakon Olesson be trusted to uphold his oath?"

"He may be trusted, my lady."

"Then Gunnar, go to the storeroom where the sheep-skins are stored. Under the skins in the back, you will find the chests." Gunnar left with Hagar to check her statement.

"Wait! There is one more question, Lady Rosamund. You say a woman may only be taken by her consent. Will you agree to be taken? I desire you."

Rosamund felt a shock course through her system and she nearly lost her balance. *If I permit him to take me, I will be spoiled as a bride. The betrothal must be cancelled with no dowry. I, a deflowered bride.*

"Haakon Olesson, you may have me, by my own consent," Rosamund assured him quietly.

"Very well, Lady Rosamund," said Haakon.

He walked up to claim his prize. As he did, he saw her eyes clearly for the first time. They were large, almost overpowering her face, and they were a blue so deep that it was almost purple. Haakon hesitated in surprise. They were the same color as the eyes of the Valkyries he had seen when Thor showed him the feast in Valhalla. There was a strangeness about Rosamund and this meeting with her, the same as there was with the golden ax. He'd best be cautious with both of them.

"Lady Rosamund, show me to your chamber. Bjorn, I leave you in charge here. Lock all these prisoners in the storehouse, and post guards outside Lady Rosamund's chamber." Knowing he needed to be cautious had not cooled his desire for her.

In her chamber, Rosamund felt as if she were naked even while she had all her clothes on. Perhaps it was the look in Haakon's eyes. If they had been hands, she would have been stripped the moment she sent Wulf away and started up the stairs with him. She hoped the people she had charged with keeping Wulf could at least prevent him from tearing apart several Norse and the fragile truce in the castle.

Haakon said nothing after Rosamund pulled the door shut behind her. He sat on the bed and started pulling off his boots. Rosamund dropped the shield and laid the dagger on top of it. Her cloak was next, then her gown. In only her shift, she bent to pull off her shoes. By the time she was finished, Haakon was looking at her again. Silently she drew her shift over her head and stood naked in front of the man. She trembled, though not only from the cold.

His eyes moved up and down her body, but with less desire rather than more. He might have been examining a new horse. *Suppose he doesn't find me pleasing? What would he do then?* She began to pray that he would, then realized what a ridiculous thing this was to pray for.

Haakon smiled. "Get into bed, or you'll be frozen."

She was startled by his concern and scrambled under the furs and lay there, rigid and ready to be taken at once. Instead Haakon stepped away from the bed and pulled off his armor. His weapons were already standing in a corner, where they would be closer to him than to either her or anyone coming through the door.

Haakon was naked when he turned to her. He still looked massive, but now he seemed far better proportioned, without the bulky armor distorting his shape. He had no wounds from tonight's battle, but plenty of bruises, and she counted half a dozen old scars. One ran across his belly and nearly into the bush of brown hair above his shaft. She had never seen a naked man and was at once terrified and aroused by his body.

Then he was in the bed beside her, his hands on her body and his lips on hers. The lips moved down her throat, and as he kissed the hollow there his beard curled around her nipples. They had been hard with the cold; now they became still harder as he kissed them. She felt as if each of them was the center of a pool of warmth flowing out in all directions through her body.

From listening to the bawdy talk of the women, she'd

had the notion that coupling was painful and unpleasant. It didn't turn out that way. She had been without affection since her mother died. Now feeling Haakon's embraces, explorations, and strokes awakened a powerful desire for more. She returned his caresses with her own and soon felt a not entirely unpleasant pain deep within her loins that could only be satisfied by the penetration of his shaft.

When the warmth and weight of Haakon's body was no longer hers, she wanted it back. She had the feeling that she'd been just about to find something enormously important and wonderfully good. She clutched the furs with both hands and arched her body, as if by tightening all her muscles she could bring back what had been snatched away at the last moment. When that didn't work, she relaxed and lay quietly on her back, staring up at the ceiling, amazed, confused.

Haakon raised himself on one elbow and looked down at Rosamund. He couldn't tell if she was asleep or not. The Valkyrie-blue eyes were wide open, but unseeing.

Gently he pulled a strand of hair away from the wide mouth, which had been so warm and eventually so eager against his. Her skin was clear enough to let him count the blue veins in her full breasts. The little nest of hair between her thighs was almost as fair as the hair on her head. He managed to get out of the bed without disturbing Rosamund, opened the door, and shouted for hot water and clean cloths. He heard someone shout a reply, and also heard a faint chorus of squeals, laughs, and mating noises. It sounded as if the castle's women were consenting in sufficient numbers to leave his men reasonably contented with their night's work.

Guthrun brought the hot water in, along with ale and bread. Haakon drank some of the ale, then climbed back into the bed to feel her warmth for a little while longer. He didn't dare spend too much time. With fatigue and satisfied desire, it would not take much to send him off to sleep.

Suddenly he found Rosamund's hands gripping him by both shoulders. Then her eyes opened, one hand stroked his cheek, and the other twined its fingers into his beard. Haakon laughed. Never before had he found himself excited by a woman's fingers in his beard. He only hoped the excitement would last. For all the strangeness in her, he was sure Rosamund would be as unhappy as any other woman if he could not offer what she was asking. Then her hand was sliding down his body. He stopped worrying about not being able to perform again because of his tiredness. He also stopped worrying about falling asleep.

Rosamund, for her part, was quickly calculating her future. It began moments before, when Haakon had gently removed the strand of hair from her lips. She had never experienced a display of tenderness from a man; she was beaten by her father and ignored by her brothers. Here was an enemy, treating her with a depth of care she had never known. *Lord Jesus, have you sent me my escape?* Rosamund considered her worth as ransom. Even if her father refused to pay, she would be free.

VIII

At last Rosamund slept.

Haakon sat up in bed and looked down at her—the tangled blond hair, the slim arm flung over the edge of the bed, the long lashes veiling the Valkyrie eyes, her breasts rising and falling steadily. He piled furs over Rosamund until only her head showed, then he forced himself to climb out of bed before he ended up sleeping as soundly as she.

He had spent longer times without a woman before this, but never had he found so much desire in himself. He also had never found a woman who asked so much of him. That Rosamund should be the woman was outside all reason, and he thought briefly and uneasily of witchcraft. He also thought even more uneasily about his sense of the gods somehow watching over Rosamund.

Then he pulled on his clothes. There was such a thing as witchcraft. There were also women with a hunger for love lying asleep in them, like piled tinder waiting for a live coal. He'd heard of them, mostly in other warriors' ale-swollen boastings and therefore rejected the stories with some doubt. Now he'd held such a woman in his arms, a woman who had been a virgin the first time he took her but who had drawn him back again and again.

By all the gods, he was even feeling ready for another

bout, just by thinking of the past ones! He laughed and bent down to kiss Rosamund's cheek. "Sleep well, you lovely little witch!" Then he straightened and gripped his dagger as a knock came on the door. "Who's there?"

"Bjorn."

The helmsman came in with a grin on his face so wide it nearly met at the back of his head. One hand was clenched into a fist.

"We've found the earl's treasure, Haakon," he said. "Three chests. The third's only been down there a few days, I'd say. And it's *gold*. Rings and chains and odd bits and pieces." Bjorn unclenched his fist and showed Haakon a ruddy piece of fine gold as long and thick as a large man's thumb. "There's a hundred more as big or bigger."

Father Odin, Thor Odinsson! Is this a joke or am I supposed to believe that our luck's really turned so much? Haakon didn't expect an answer, but he hoped the gods would at least recognize a serious question. That much gold would build and man two ships the size of *Wave Walker*, with enough leftover provisions and armor to leave Olaf Haraldsson shaking with fear.

"And the other chests?"

"Mostly silver and bronze, a little copper. And there's more silver in the cups and—"

Haakon raised a hand for silence. He thought he had heard a horn sounding from the walls, but perhaps it was just a trick of the wind. He finished pulling on his tunic and picked up his chain mail, handing it to Bjorn. "Help me on with this."

Then he stopped. A battle horn was sounding. A moment later he heard booted feet pounding along the hall below, toward the stairs.

"Haakon! Haakon!" It was Gunnar's voice.

"Up here!"

The poet burst in through the door, a spear in one hand and his left arm and chest spattered with blood. He took in Haakon's startled look and smiled grimly.

"Not my blood, Haakon. I've been settling one or two debts from my slavery here. I challenged them fairly, so there's been no oath-breaking. The English are coming. Turo the Finn's just brought in the men from the farm with the word."

"The prisoners?"

"He brought most of them in. From what Turo says, Harud Olafsson is leading the English."

Haakon thrust his head into the mail shirt and shook himself until it settled comfortably onto his shoulders. Then he picked up his helmet and the golden ax. "Bjorn, gather all our English in the great hall and keep them there until I send orders."

Rosamund was fully awakened by the conference. When Bjorn and Gunnar left her chambers, she threw off the furs and looked at Haakon expectantly.

"Rosamund, who is this Harud Olafsson?"

"He is the man to whom I will be betrothed. He is a fearful and wicked man and is said to have the evil eye. We are supp—"

"Who is his father?"

"Another demon, Olaf Haralds—"

"Bjorn!" Haakon yelled. "Rosamund, get dressed." Haakon took hold of his ax and stormed from the room in search of his helmsman.

Turo the Finn met Haakon and Gunnar as they came out of the hall into the narrow passage leading to the gate in the inner wall. Most of the passage was already filled with the prisoners from the farm, sitting or squatting with their hands bound, their feet hobbled with thongs or rags, and looks of raw fear on their faces.

"Where's Thorkell?" Haakon asked. He had been left in command at the farm. In spite of his temper, Thorkell was also brave and a shrewd leader in battle.

"I don't know," said Turo. "When we saw the English coming, he told me to take these—" a thumb jerked at the prisoners, "and our wounded, and come to you. Black Ayolf goes with him, and both take bows."

"Did you lose any of the prisoners?"

A shrug. "Don't know. If so, we didn't talk where they could hear, so they don't know much about us to tell their friends."

"Good." Thorkell and Turo had done well. The prisoners couldn't be left to add their strength to the English attack, particularly when this might be the only attack Haakon's men would have to face before their ships came around to bring them away.

Haakon took out the piece of gold that Bjorn had showed him, broke it in half, and gave one piece to Turo. "The other half's for Thorkell, when he comes back."

"I thank you." The Finn bobbed his head and went off toward the ladder up the rear of the inner wall.

"I hope Thorkell doesn't kill Harud," said Haakon. "If he really is leading the English, I want to take him for myself."

"Have you fought him before?" Gunnar asked.

"No. But I've wanted to. This Harud Olafsson is Olaf Haraldsson's son. It is his wyrd that led him to our gate now my luck has changed."

The horn sounded again, and someone shouted, "It's Thorkell and—no, it's just Black Ayolf."

Another shout. "Where's Thorkell?"

A gasping cry from outside the wall, barely loud enough to hear. "They—Thorkell's taken. He told me to come in—"

Haakon cursed briefly. "You, you, you—" he pointed at three men "—go out and get Ayolf. Then make sure there's no one left in the outer defenses." His orders to stay in the castle had been strict, but there were always a few fools who strayed like sheep, looking for booty they wouldn't have to share or a dark corner for tumbling a girl.

The men dashed out through the gate. Haakon cupped his hands and shouted up at the top of the inner wall. "Hagar, do you have your fire arrows?"

"Yes, Haakon."

"Keep them ready." He'd keep his promise to Rosamund if he could, but he might have to set a few thatched roofs on fire to give his men light for the fighting.

"Gunnar, tell Bjorn to take all the people in the hall and put them in one of the storehouses. We won't have to worry about them that way. Rosamund and her women can stay upstairs in the hall if they have no weapons."

"And the treasure?"

"Have Bjorn take it to the edge of the cliff. Count off six men, three from each ship, to guard it. They stay by it until the battle's over, unless you, I, Bjorn, or Knut One-Eye sends word to you that the battle's lost. Then they throw it off the cliff into the sea." From all Haakon had seen tonight, Knut could be trusted in this, and in any case not trusting him could make for bad blood after the fight. "If we do go down, Harud won't get much good from it, with his dowry gold down among the whales."

"Too bad we wouldn't be hearing what he says when he learns it," said Gunnar. "He'll scream like a man being gelded." He hurried off, clearing English prisoners and an occasional Norseman out of his path with his spear. Haakon ran to the ladder and scrambled up on to the rickety walkway around the inner wall of Edmund's Hold.

Rosamund's first movements made her aware of the pains in her thighs and between her legs. She dressed hurriedly and set aside some clothing in case Haakon decided to take her with him. Then the chamber door flew open and the Norse drove her maids inside and closed the door behind them.

The women were calmer than they had been earlier when the first word came of Norse approaching the castle. Guthrun said Rosamund's brother Mark had come back, and Harud with him. Between them, they might have enough men to retake the castle.

Mother Mary, tell me what to wish for, if you can't tell me what to do. Will Harud's evil eye protect him against the Norse? Lord Jesus, please do not let anything happen to Haakon and—Rosamund suddenly broke off, startled by her thoughts. Her brother was in this siege, and yet she was praying for the safety of a Viking raider over that of her own kin. Mark was likely to hurl himself impetuously at the wall, dying on Viking spears with nothing to show for it.

Mark was only two years older than she. She couldn't say she had much more affection for him than for Oswain and Wilfrid, but she'd certainly had fewer quarrels with him. He was young enough not to have hardened into cruelty and sullen bad temper. He was also young enough to think of little more than proving his manhood in bed, in drinking, and in battle. No one, least of all Rosamund, would be surprised if Mark never saw twenty. He might even die tonight if Harud did not hold him back.

But if he were held back, Mark's hot blood would overflow in another direction. There might be harsh words between him and Harud, perhaps blows. Then they would be at blood-feud. The idea was mildly amusing, since her father, Earl Edmund, was the man least fit to play peacemaker.

She had to get out of here. Whatever she might eventually do or say, she couldn't do it shut up here. Rosamund peered through the largest crack in the door and saw the stairs unguarded. She tested the door. It was unlocked. The Norse apparently expected fear to keep her and the women in this chamber during the battle.

"I'm going out to see what can be done," Rosamund said. "The rest of you, stay here."

"But, lady, will you go out unguarded?" asked Guthrun. She was pale, but dry eyed and almost successful in keeping her hands and voice steady.

"No, I'll find Wulf." *If they haven't killed him for their sport*, she thought. "And the Norse will take him more seriously than they would any of you. This is our work, mine and Wulf's."

She sat down to tug on her shoes and briefly considered if she should try escaping from the castle. After a moment she decided that there was no way out and no purpose even if she found a way. If the Norse lost the wall, there'd be no escape. If they held it, the only way to freedom was along the cliffs, where Wulf and the maids could never follow her safely.

Also, there was the matter of standing by her people—and they were her responsibility. She hadn't sworn not to try escaping, but she knew that trying would anger Haakon. He seemed like a just man, but would his sense of justice survive his rage when he found her gone? If only she knew his plans for her, she would know what to do.

She forced herself to her feet. In another moment her courage might fail her. Without saying a word to the women or hearing a word they said to her, she slipped out the door.

As she set foot on the stairs, she heard a man's scream float over the walls on the wind.

Haakon made no effort to hold the outer wall. That would be spreading his men too thin. It would also mean leaving the prisoners too far in his rear, not under his eye or in reach of his hand.

The English were quick to find where the Vikings had felled the three logs, and before long Harud's men were gathered in the yard before the inner wall. Half-hidden by darkness and the shadows of the buildings, they were hard to count, but Haakon guessed there were at least seventy or eighty.

Not impossible odds, with care and courage.

Haakon raised the golden ax in both hands and felt its warmth increase the strength in his arms. Assured of their path, he then called to the men on either side, "Hold, until we see if they've any surprises for us."

Two torches flared in the darkness below, showing a broad-framed, red-faced man and a slender youth with an astonishing shock of pale hair. Both were armed, and there was a blanket-shrouded form at their feet.

"Haakon Olesson!" the younger man shouted. "Are you there?"

"That's Mark Edmundsson, the third son," said Gunnar's voice beside Haakon. "I'd hoped he and Harud would quarrel."

"Hope sharpens no swords," said Haakon, then watched Mark bend to pull the blanket from the man on the ground. It was Thorkell, just recognizable under the blood from the wounds left by a dozen kinds of torture. Even worse, he was still alive; Haakon saw him blink at the torchlight. Thorkell must have told the English the name of the man who had taken the castle.

"Haakon!" shouted Harud. "Are you man enough to show yourself or are you a coward like your father?"

"Ask your bride if Haakon's man enough!" shouted someone. Rough laughter rolled along the wall.

Harud's face twisted cruelly, and he drew a knife. Mark gripped his shoulder, but he shook off the young man's hand, then knelt and slashed twice between Thorkell's legs. No one who heard Thorkell's cry would ever forget it before his own dying day or forget the sight of Thorkell arching his mutilated body until the blood pouring out of him took away the last of his strength and he fell back into a puddle of reddish mud.

"Come out and fight like men," roared Harud. "Come out, and you'll die like men. Make us come after you, and you'll die like this one here!"

Haakon's blood drained from his face, then flowed back up so violently, he thought his head would explode. He turned to Bjorn. "Bring me a prisoner. A man."

Bjorn turned to do his bidding and returned with a man in his twenties, already crying in terror of his unknown fate.

"Tie him up," Haakon directed grimly, and picked up his ax. "I want his legs spread."

The man's crying turned to sobbing, incoherent pleas for mercy. Haakon deafened himself to the sobs; this act he owed to Thorkell. Haakon bent over the man thrashing wildly in avoidance of the ax. Haakon closed his eyes, wanting only a mind's picture of Thorkell's torment, not this Englishman's.

Suddenly the ax turned bitterly cold in his grip. His palm and fingers nearly flew off the handle to stave the biting pain. The ax clattered onto the battlement floor, next to the prisoner.

"Let him go," Haakon ordered. The man's crying took hold in earnest, and he was dragged back into the storehouse.

"You will die, Saxon!" shouted Turo. He seemed torn between rage and scorn. Someone else replied with an arrow. It wasn't Hagar—he never shot without orders, and seldom at such an uncertain target. Mark Edmundsson twisted with a serpent's grace and speed, catching the arrow on his shield. Then he raised his sword.

"At them!"

The English swarmed toward the wall. Haakon cupped his hands. "Hagar! The fire arrows!" A tiny comet arched through the darkness, and fire spread into the dry thatch. The light showed at least sixty Englishmen, all of them running. One band carried a ladder to scale the wall, another carried a heavy beam from the carpenter's shed as a makeshift battering ram.

"Hold fast!" Haakon roared. "We've got the numbers to

beat them, and we've got the wall as well. Hold these and
there are no more to come at us tonight! Hold these, and
our road home is sure!"

Another burning roof added its light to the battlefield.
The English were at the wall. It had no ditch and was so
low that a man standing on another's shoulders could
reach the top and pull himself up. That is, he could do this
if Haakon's defenders on top let him.

Harud Olafsson led the men with the beam toward the
gate. Mark Edmundsson paced back and forth along the
wall, five men forming a small shield wall around him as
he moved. Then he raised his sword and all six rushed
toward the wall. At its foot the five shield men knelt, four
of them holding one shield flat. Mark sprang on to the
shield, its bearers sagging under his weight, then he rose
up the wall. His sword whirled, ruining the face of an
incautious Norseman who leaned over too far.

Then one of Hagar's arrows found its mark in Mark's
buttocks. He howled like a mad ghost and danced so
wildly that one of the shield-bearers lost his grip. The
shield tilted and Mark kept from falling only by gripping
the nearest log. Then a spear was thrust down at him. He
ducked, lost his balance, and went down with a crash and
a stream of curses on all Norse. The spearman brought
down one of Mark's shield-bearers, but the other four
managed to drag him away from the wall and out of the
fight.

By then the men with the improvised ram were hard at
work. Harud Olafsson strode back and forth, urging the
men on, ordering others to hold their shields over the
men on the ram. Haakon studied Harud and his men with
interest. A good opponent was always prepared, and thus

more dangerous. Haakon wanted to be ready when he avenged his family's honor. Songs would be written about Ole Ketilsson's son Haakon restoring dignity to his kin.

Then Haakon was abruptly reminded that a warrior has to survive a battle to hear the songs sung about it. An English head rose up over the wall, and the man's spear missed Haakon by the thickness of a cat's whiskers. He swung his ax sideways, knocking the Englishman off his perch on a comrade's shoulders. Haakon shifted his grip on the ax to give himself the longest possible two-handed reach. To his relief, the ax was warm again in his hands, but he wished he had brought his shield. There had to be archers out there who would be shooting as soon as the Norse beat back the first rush.

The ram still thudded and crashed against the gate, and Haakon wondered how long it would hold. Its timbers were stout enough, but its hinges were wretched affairs, one of them only a mass of leather thongs. Barrels and bales from the storehouses were piled up behind the gate, but if it came off its hinges—

Craaaaakkk! Haakon heard the shudder of the gate over the roar of the battle. "Knut!" he shouted. "Down on the ground and hold the gate! Take all the men you need." If all the men on the ram got through the gateway, the Norse on the wall would be caught between two fires. Then the English might release the prisoners, surround their enemies, and give them the choice of dying in battle or dying like Thorkell the Scarred. Suddenly this night held the promise of sending many good men to Valhalla to no purpose. Should he send word to Gunnar to have the treasure thrown off the cliff?

No. Let's wait until there's no other way left to strike at the English. He was sure that even if he were the only man left on his feet, he could still cut his way through the English with the golden ax and reach the treasure in time to snatch it forever out of Edmund's hands.

Another English head rose over the wall. Haakon and Turo attacked it at the same moment. The Englishman swung his sword at Turo, not hurting him but forcing him to turn outward. But an arrow from below found a weakness in Turo's leather jacket. He died where he stood, not even trying to pluck the arrow out of his chest before he fell backward off the wall.

Haakon loosed a roar and brought the golden ax down with a superhuman strength. Suddenly the English swordsman had no head. As he went over backward, he knocked the man on the ladder behind him to the ground. For a moment there was no one on the ladder. Haakon dropped the ax to the walkway, seized the ladder with both hands, and heaved. It flew over his head, crashing to the ground inside the wall. The archer who'd killed Turo sent an arrow at Haakon, but it miraculously clanged off the head of the golden ax as Haakon raised it again.

Then he heard Knut's voice shouting, "Haakon! To the gate!" Haakon ran along the wall, dodging arrows, until he was right above the gateway. Harud's men were struggling through it and scrambling over the planks of the gate and the barrels and sacks behind it. Some of Harud's men were going down, as were some of the Norse in their path.

Haakon leaped down into the middle of the English attackers. He knocked a man over with the sheer weight of his impact, brought a foot down on the man's back, and felt the spine crack. He screamed, Haakon turned, and the golden ax put an end to the screaming. He saw that

the ax was glowing, light pouring out of the head ev
though it was now dripping with English blood.

Then Haakon was challenged by a small Englishma
who ran toward him, bobbing and weaving away from the
ax. Haakon swung again, the Englishman sprang aside,
and the ax stove in a barrel. Ale gushed out, turning the
ground slick under the Englishman's feet. The next time
he tried to avoid the golden ax his feet slipped in the ooze
and the ax caught him in the thigh. Knut came up beside
Haakon and drove a spear into the Englishman's chest.

The two of them stood for a moment against half a dozen
English. Then Gunnar joined them, and a moment later
Bjorn came up. Then more Norsemen were defending the
gateway. The English were all down, and a slim blond
figure was scrambling alone over the wreckage and the
bodies toward Haakon. In spite of his wound in the
buttocks, Mark Edmundsson had returned to the fray.

What happens if I kill Rosamund's brother? He was
determined not to let anyone else close with Mark
Edmundsson, and opened his mouth to order his men
back. Then an arrow took Mark in the leg, and Haakon
heard Hagar's cry of triumph. Three Englishmen darted
forward to grip their chief as he staggered, then dragged
him cursing back out through the gateway. They were
beaten!

Where was Harud Olafsson? Now that the Norse had
the advantage, Olafsson had vanished.

As Mark's curses died away, a new noise cut through
them and the dying battle sounds outside the wall. Somewhere in the darkness behind Haakon, a dog was barking
furiously.

*   *   *

Rosamund had an easy way down the stairs into the hall. Then she slipped along the wall like a mouse, ready to hide under a bench or behind a pillar at the mere sound of a man. At the same time she searched the darkness for some sort of weapon. This was easier for her than for most people. Ever since she was a child she could see in the dark like a cat.

She found a spear discarded by one of her people at the same moment Wulf found her. He let out one joyful bark before she quieted him. Then she pulled him behind a pillar and leaned against it, holding her breath, wishing she could silence her beating heart. She was desperately glad Wulf was with her again, and at the same time listened fearfully for men drawn by Wulf's bark.

None came. In silence Rosamund and her dog reached the main door. It was unlocked and unguarded. As she pushed it open, trying not to draw a squeal from the hinges, the uproar of battle poured over her like the incoming tide. Harud and Mark were leading their men straight against the wall.

Just what I'd expect of them, she thought. She felt angry at them for thinking of nothing better, and angry at herself because she had devised no better plan.

All the Norse seemed to be on the wall, except a handful she saw standing on the edge of the cliff. A torch was struck into the ground at their feet, and by its light she saw the chests of her father's treasure. Haakon seemed to be thinking of everything, including how to be sure an English victory would be barren.

The servant women had spoken of "our people in the big storehouse," but Rosamund would have known where the English prisoners were without that. Timbers, barrels, and sacks were piled up in front of the door to nearly her own height. She stood with a hand on Wulf's collar. For a moment she wasn't sure where to go next, then saw that the far side of the pile at the door was hidden from view of the Norse guarding the treasure.

The noise of the battle rose higher. Words she caught amid the shouting told her that Mark and Harud had the gate down, that Englishmen were coming through, and that suddenly the battle now might go against the Norse. A man who'd been sitting on one of the treasure chests jumped up, his boot brushed against the torch, it fell over and went out.

Rosamund jerked up her skirts and in the sudden darkness dashed across the open ground. Wulf loped after her without any command. If she could just get the storehouse door clear before the men noticed her, then let some of the prisoners out into the rear of the Norse . . .

Under her breath, she cursed herself for not thinking to bring more weapons. The first few prisoners to come out would be meeting armed men with their bare hands.

She dragged away the blockage, but stopped when she came to a barrel that must have taken all the strength of two men to move. She could not budge it by herself. She needed a lever.

She started looking for a piece of timber, no longer worrying about noise. The battle was making such a din that she could have shouted, beaten a drum, or chopped down the door with an ax without the men who were guarding the treasure hearing her. She found a suitable

piece of timber and was wedging it under the barrel when
one of Haakon's men walked around the pile and saw her.

He was obviously drunk and he had his trousers pulled
down. For a moment he only stared owlishly at Rosamund,
and in that moment Wulf leaped at him. He was sober
enough to bring his arm up, which saved his throat from
Wulf's teeth. He went over backward with a thud, and
Wulf landed on his chest, growling and worrying at the
man's arm while the Norseman frantically tried to grip the
dog's collar.

Rosamund ran to the struggling pair and brought the
timber down on the man's skull. He went limp, but two
more Vikings ran up. One of them screamed as Wulf's
teeth sank into his thigh, but the other came on. He didn't
draw his weapon, though, and Rosamund knew the look in
his eyes. He was confident he could take her barehanded,
then rape her and tell Haakon that what she had done
made her fair prey.

His hand closed on her shoulder. She jerked back, and
her gown tore. The upper part of the garment stayed in
the man's hands, and the falling skirt tangled her feet at
the next step. Rosamund went down, and the man howled
in triumph. But she swung the wood at his groin, and he
howled with a very different note in his voice. She swung
again, and one leg crumpled under him. He went to his
knees as she rose, and a third swing stretched him on the
ground.

"Wulf! Here!" The dog ran back to her side, as she
picked up her spear. Three more Vikings ran up and she
saw the look in their eyes and would have prayed except
that her throat was too dry to do it out loud and her mind
too blank to do it silently.

*   *   *

If the battle at the gate had lasted much longer, Haakon would have found Rosamund sprawled on the ground under one of his men. Not long after that he might have found her dead. As it was, he ran up just as the three men were moving in, shields ready against her spear or Wulf's teeth, but otherwise clearly intending to keep her alive until they'd used her thoroughly.

"Hold there!" shouted Haakon. The three men turned to face him.

"Why? This bitch " began one.

Haakon dropped the golden ax, closed with the speaker, and drove one fist hard into his stomach, another into his jaw. As he went down Haakon gripped the other two by the neck and heaved. Both fell

"When I say hold, you obey first, talk afterwards."

"The bitch and her dog—"

Haakon raised the golden ax, and one of the men drew his knife. Things might have become ugly if Bjorn, Knut, and three others had not run up. Haakon pointed at the three would-be rapists.

"Take them away. They can have their shares for the night's work, but they leave us after that."

"And them?" Bjorn pointed at Rosamund, standing in a dress hanging by one shoulder, and Wulf, who looked like a demon in the shape of a dog, his eyes three times normal size, his jaws bloody.

Haakon looked at the injured men on the ground. They were groaning and starting to stir. Rosamund's fingers were bone-white in their grip on her spear. The Valkyrie-purple eyes met his without blinking. He shifted the ax to his left hand and held out his right to the growling dog.

"Here, Wulf. Here, boy! Come to me!" Wulf's ears twitched and he rose, licking his muzzle. Rosamund's eyes flickered down to the dog, her breath caught, and her face turned as pale as her fingers. The dog looked up at her, uncertain.

"Come, Wulf!" The dog took two cautious steps, then went across to Haakon and gazed at him. Haakon smiled. "Good dog." He rested a hand on the shaggy head. "Now sit down!" A gentle tug on the collar brought Wulf around to his side. "Good dog," he repeated. Wulf shook himself and sat down.

He saw Knut and some of the others fingering amulets at neck or belt, but ignored them. "Now, Lady Rosamund—" he began. The Valkyrie eyes rolled up, showing white, and the slim body gave way like an overtight bowstring breaking. Rosamund fell forward, and Haakon caught her. He pressed a hand to her breast to be sure she was alive.

He lifted her. "Bjorn, take the lady to her chamber, and keep her there. Knut, find me some ale and some food."

When Rosamund awoke, the room spun slowly, blurred slightly, then came to rest, focused. Guthrun was on the bed, holding her hand and wiping her brow with a cold cloth.

"My lady, are you sick?"

Rosamund smiled bleakly. It had all been too much for her in too little time: first the attack, then Haakon, then the counterattack, and lastly, Wulf. That had been the final blow. "Guthrun, I am well enough. But—I have no place here now."

"My lady, this is your home."

"Do you remember when I first brought Wulf home? Do you remember the priest?"

Guthrun nodded. The dog who now weighed more than she and who could tear the throat from a bear was once a little puppy, given to Rosamund by an Irish priest.

"I know where that dog comes from," the priest had told Rosamund before he died. "I can't tell you, but I know. Trust him more than any of your blood to see the way you should go, for he's got a better heart than any of them. If he follows another's voice, look closely at that man or woman. You'll see something worth finding—worth holding."

"Guthrun, Wulf went to Haakon's side at his command. The priest said it would be a sign, but I *never* expected Wulf would obey a Viking."

Rosamund fell silent, and Guthrun considered what she had heard. If Rosamund's priest had said Wulf had seeing eyes, he had probably spoken the truth. Guthrun knew the White Christ was a powerful god who gave the *papas* or priests who served him wisdom and power.

"What will you tell Haakon?"

"I will tell him none of this. But I must leave with him when it is time. Perhaps he will take me for ransom, then I will make myself useful and he will permit me to stay."

"What of your betrothal? And your father?"

"Guthrun, please. You are the only person I would hate to leave. But maybe you will be able to accompany me. Now that Gunnar is serving Haakon, I might be able to convince you to come?"

Guthrun blushed deeply, just as Rosamund had expected.

"Not a word of this, Guthrun, to anyone!"

Guthrun nodded as she considered these unexpected

new prospects and left the chamber, having completely forgotten to ask leave to do so from her mistress.

IX

When Haakon finished eating, it was still dark. Fog was rolling in from the sea, and as he made his rounds among the men, the fog grew steadily thicker, and the surf beating on the rocks at the foot of the Ram's Head fell almost silent. The fog was hauntingly ominous to the Norse, whom it kept from escaping by sea.

Haakon found most of the men hard at work. There were twelve wounded to be tended, and five dead to be laid out. Guards were mounted on the wall, at the treasure chests, and with the prisoners in the storehouse.

"Some of the men aren't easy in their minds about this fog," said Bjorn. He lowered his voice. "And I've heard talk of witchcraft."

"The ax?" Haakon asked.

"No. I do not believe its light is visible to anyone but you. But they say magic lets you conjure that dog Wulf to your side and that the English witch is fighting back with this fog."

Haakon couldn't help wondering what Bjorn might say about magic if he knew of the night on the island and the message from Thor. "Anything more than talk?"

"Not yet. But I think the men would be happier if you sacrificed one or two of the Englishmen to Odin."

Haakon shook his head. "We've sworn not to harm the people. I'll not be an oath-breaker merely to quiet a few fears."

"Did the English hold back from harming us?"

"They've done nothing to make a sacrifice lawful." Haakon's voice held an edge. Making such a decision was one matter. Making sure no one defied him was another. He could not leave the question here.

"Did the English have any horses in the stables?"

"Yes. Six or seven."

"Good. I'll make the horse sacrifice. Spread this word among the men."

"I will." Bjorn turned away and vanished into the fog. Even holding a torch, Haakon could see barely half a ship's length. *Red Hawk* and *Wave Walker* would not be coming to the Ram's Head until the fog lifted. However, this fact wouldn't be altered by his worrying about it. He turned his mind elsewhere.

There would be no sacrifice of Englishmen if he could help it. Such a sacrifice seemed to him like oath-breaking. It also seemed unwise, at least until he knew what to believe about that night on the island. The golden ax was real. So was Rosamund—and was she part of his first task for the masters of Valhalla?

He would have to give some more thought to Rosamund. She had never been entirely out of his mind since he awoke. If he took her home with him, there would be men to say he was bringing a spaewife among them, one who held no love for the Norse. This could mean some danger to him, more to her. It would also very probably mean harsh words with his mother, Lady Sigrid—and Haakon's guts writhed like snakes at the thought.

He badly wanted more of Rosamund's company. Standing there in the cold fog, he felt warm as he thought of her.

Haakon retraced his steps to the great hall and hurried up the stairs to the door of Rosamund's chamber. The guards let him in, and a few sharp words drove out all the servants except Guthrun. She stood by the bed where Rosamund lay asleep.

"You too," he said. "Out."

She shook her head. "I stay with my lady!" Guthrun's eyes were a pale ice-blue rather than the near purple of Rosamund's, but they held much the same look. *A warrior in woman's form just like her mistress—a spearman standing by his chief in the face of death.*

Haakon glared. What he had to say to Rosamund should not be heard by others.

"Woman, are you wise to speak to me this way?"

"Perhaps not. But what can you Vikings do to me you haven't done already, without breaking the oath you swore to my lady?"

The women of Edmund's Hold, it seemed to Haakon, had the courage of berserkers and the nimble tongues of lawspeakers at a Thing. He found himself admiring Guthrun's courage when Rosamund spoke: "Guthrun, you may go." Her voice was low but clear and steady.

When Haakon finally spoke, it was more harshly than he'd intended.

"Lady Rosamund, you will be aboard my ship when we sail today. You and your dog. We'll take him, too."

She sat up, and her thin, pale face became a mask. She had a delicate balance to maintain, wanting to go with Haakon while giving him the impression that she did not.

The furs slipped away from her shoulders, and Haakon saw dark purple bruises. When she spoke again, only the movement of her lips broke the mask.

"I am not forsworn, Haakon. I gave you the castle, its treasures, and . . . myself. I swore to do nothing else. What about you and your oath that you'd burn nothing? Last night your archers—"

"Before I ever met you, I took an oath to lead my men well. I would have led them badly if I hadn't ordered the fires set."

"That does not change the fact that you broke your oath—"

"Enough talk of oaths! Prepare yourself for the voyage. We can take only two chests of your belongings, so choose carefully. We will also take your maid."

"Only if Guthrun consents. Swear that you will not force her."

Haakon rested his right hand on the ax handle. "I swear by this ax and by my own honor." It was a small thing to do to remove a large obstacle to Rosamund's coming with him.

"Good."

Haakon felt like a young spearman, standing to learn whether he'd been judged fit to join a chief's band. Anger rose in him as he wondered if a good thrashing would at least blunt Rosamund's tongue for the rest of the voyage home. She had no right to expect him to come to her terms.

"Are you prime-signed?" she asked.

Prime-signing was a ceremony performed on men from lands where the people did not follow the White Christ. It did not make a man a Christian, but it made it lawful for

Christians to deal with him. Haakon had been prime-
signed as a boy in Ireland, and had found it vastly useful in
his trading.

"Yes. You haven't damned yourself by dealing with me."

"No." More softly, "Not by that." Rosamund managed to
pale and conjured tears in her eyes.

"You're afraid you've damned yourself by coming to my
bed?"

She nodded. "I may be forgiven, because I did it for my
people, not for my own lust." Haakon managed not to
laugh. "But it is a sin, nonetheless."

"So I've heard the *papas* say," said Haakon with a shrug.
"And you've damned yourself without any need."

The mask on her face shivered. "What?"

"I wasn't going to slaughter and burn here no matter
what you did or refused to do. So you came to me when
you didn't need to, and enjoyed what you didn't have to
do."

The mask shivered again, then broke. "You—you louse-
bitten whoremongering rutting lying—*Norse!*" She sputtered
like a pot overflowing into the fire, unable to think of any
worse name to call him. Then she picked up her wadded
shift, hurled it at him, reached out of the bed to snatch up
one shoe, and hurled it. Her aim was good and that slim
arm was surprisingly strong. The shoe struck Haakon
across the bridge of the nose, hard enough to sting and
make his eyes water. A finger's breath to the left or the
right, and he might have been like Knut One-Eye.

He reached the bed as she snatched up the second
shoe; he gripped her wrist and squeezed until she dropped
the shoe. Then he reached over and caught her by the hair
with his free hand, pulling her head back.

He slapped her hard with his free hand. Her cheek was as red as her lips, but she didn't make a sound.

He reached down and jerked the furs away from her so she sat naked before him, one hand stroking her cheek. Although Haakon believed her tumble had been unnecessary, Rosamund had been well aware that it would dissolve her betrothal agreement. Now that Haakon was taking her with him, her bedding him would have been only a matter of time anyway. She was certainly safe now, and she experienced an overwhelming joy and relief. Haakon would never know how well he fell into her plans.

For a moment the mask was back. Then it broke, not in tears but in a smile, which turned into a giggle. The giggle turned into laughter, and Haakon glared. Rosamund lay back and laughed, holding one hand over her belly and the other over her breasts. Those breasts moved interestingly as she laughed; by the time Rosamund stopped laughing, he was lying in bed beside her and pulling her toward him.

Haakon couldn't recall a time when a bedding begun so badly had ended so well. He roused himself from the edge of sleep when he heard a horn blowing on the wall and Bjorn's voice calling for the change of guards.

Did she draw me back by witchcraft, as the men say? Or do we have a sign from Freya, the goddess of love—or perhaps from Thor in a bawdy mood?

He didn't know. He did know that he was old enough to be needing a wife. He also knew that if he wanted beauty to light his house, wisdom to manage it, joy to warm his bed, and courage to breed into his sons begotten in that bed, he did not need to look farther than Rosamund.

Time to answer this when we're home. He went down the stairs, pinning his cloak up as he went. Outside the fog was as thick as ever. They still could not leave. Haakon wondered how many of his men might now be thinking of the human sacrifice to Odin.

At dawn, the fog began to thin out under a light but steady breeze. Before the guards were changed again, the fog was lifting. Knut led a dozen men into the outer castle to make a final search and found three Englishmen who'd crept into the shelter of the unburned buildings, too frightened or too badly hurt to flee with their comrades. Olafsson, Edmundsson, and the surviving attackers were gone. From the outer wall Knut saw the tracks of men and horses, but not a single living Englishman.

Bjorn set to work getting the booty and the new passengers ready for loading aboard the ships. There were ten able-bodied English prisoners who had been taken in the night's fighting, and six Norse thralls who had been set free. There were the chests of coins, several bales of cloth, and more fine vessels and decorated weapons and armor.

"If there were much more, I'd really be praying for fine weather on the way home," said Bjorn. "We'll be heavy-laden as it is, for shorthanded ships." His unspoken question was, *What about the sacrifice?*

Haakon felt that questions left unspoken could also be left unanswered. "Make sure you've got plenty of thongs and ropes for carrying the wounded down the cliff," he said. "The path's no trouble for the able-bodied, but we'd best be ready to help the wounded. Save some rope for a leash for the dog. I want him carefully lowered down the cliff if he doesn't come willingly with Lady Rosamund."

Bjorn nodded and turned away.

Gunnar was next to come up, a smile on his thin face. "Rosamund's maid Guthrun will come with her lady," he said.

"You mean she's coming with you?"

"Well—yes. At least that's the way I see it, although she doesn't quite see it so yet. But after we get home, if you keep me in your service—"

"I will, if you wish to stay."

"I do, and Guthrun is one of the reasons. She has Norse blood, and I think she'll find a better home among us than at the Ram's Head."

"I think a louse would find a better home elsewhere," said Haakon. "Very well. But no forcing her."

Gunnar looked as if he'd been slapped and said what had to be the first thing he thought. "Has Rosamund put a spell on your wits?"

Haakon also nearly spoke his first thoughts. *From the others I'd expect such fool's words, but from you? . . .* Then he remembered that Gunnar was a poet who might see farther than other men, and that he'd asked an understandable question and deserved the same sort of answer.

"Guthrun is doing an honorable thing, standing by her lady this way," Haakon said. "It would bring ill luck to us if she were to suffer for it. As for Rosamund's spells, she's done nothing to my wits—or as some think, to the weather."

By noon the fog was gone, and the sails of the two longships were in sight. The breeze had risen until the rocks at the foot of the cliff were spray-slick and treacherous. Haakon went out to the stables to choose the horses for the sacrifice to Odin.

By the time the two ships were off the Ram's Head, the breeze was so strong that Snorri needed to have all his

men aboard to keep the ships off the rocks with oars. So
Haakon sacrificed the two horses with only the survivors
of the battle watching him. Gunnar chanted, and Bjorn
held the horses, Haakon stunned them with the golden ax,
and Knut cut their throats. *Now,* thought Haakon, *there is
only one band of men following me, not two*.

And if Odin thinks otherwise, let him say so.

As Gunnar chanted, each man except Haakon sang or
spoke his own wishes and hopes. Haakon found that he
could not say out loud what came from farthest inside him.

*Let what there is between me and Rosamund be strong
and lawful, so that it may grow and endure*.

He got no answer to that from the gods, or from
Rosamund. By the time they loaded the ships, the mask
was back on her face. She neither spoke nor smiled as she
and Wulf went below, into the low space beneath *Wave
Walker*'s afterdeck. She stayed there as the two ships beat
their way offshore to where the wind would take them
south. She was still below as the Ram's Head and Edmund's
Hold faded from sight astern.

X

Gunnar Thorsten's "Song of Haakon" told of the good
weather and the high spirits of everyone aboard *Red Hawk*
and *Wave Walker* as they sailed for home. This was the
truth as far as he knew it, but he didn't know everything.

Only Bjorn knew Rosamund troubled Haakon, and he

hoped that Haakon would decide Rosamund's fate before she gave Bjorn and his chief a reason to quarrel. No woman was worth the sacrifice of a comradeship hammered out over years, in battle, storm, and feasting hall. Unfortunately Haakon was not a man to babble of anything as close to his heart as this must be. The best-intentioned words from Bjorn could not change that, so all he could do was hope.

Haakon knew Bjorn's thoughts better than he let the man know. He also had more doubts about Rosamund than he cared to admit. Was she a witch, as some of his men suspected? He no longer feared Rosamund's casting some spell to bring shipwreck or pirates on his men. If she could not keep the fog over the Ram's Head or stop the horse sacrifice, she could hardly do anything worth fearing even if she wanted to. Besides, he had heard that such witchery was unlawful for Christian women.

He was less certain about Rosamund's powers over himself. He silenced many of the mutterings and a few of his own doubts by taking one of the captured thrall-women from *Wave Walker* to his bed three nights in succession. After that he could at least be sure that Rosamund had done nothing to bind him to her or take away his manhood.

Neither did Haakon know that Rosamund cried herself to sleep those three nights at sea. No one knew that except Guthrun, who threw poisonous looks at all the Norse and wished she could hurl something more solid. Gunnar only knew that the maid seemed to be turning her back on him every time he wanted to talk to her.

Off the Frisian coast a northwest gale sprang up to drive them landward. When it died away they were close to shore, and Haakon decided to seek a landing place for a few days of hot food and dry beds.

They found one with a stream of clean water and a marsh teeming with waterfowl close by. There they met Ragnar the Noseless with his longship, *Whale's King*, and a fat trading *knarr*. Like Haakon, Ragnar had fought in Odo's host before Paris, and Haakon knew him for an honest if somewhat lazy man. He also knew that this meeting would be the first test of how *Wave Walker*'s men would behave among other Norsemen.

If Ragnar learned anything that he should not have known, it was not from *Wave Walker*'s men. They told a story of how Leatherbreeches had died in a desperate battle, and Haakon had come along, rallying them and leading them on a successful raid. After this the leaderless men of *Wave Walker* had decided to follow Haakon home. Some of them might even sail with him next year.

They were silent about the details of the raid on the Ram's Head and said nothing about Haakon's great booty or the men Haakon had punished for their treatment of Rosamund. Ragnar's men might be honest, but they might also talk where pirates could hear them, and before Haakon was safely home.

Ragnar had spent most of the summer trading among the Norse settlements in the Bay of the Seine and had acquired a fair amount of cargo. Now he was bound for Hedeby in Denmark to sell his cargo and stay the winter there. Haakon decided to turn *Red Hawk*'s cargo from Iceland over to Ragnar. It would fetch a better price from the merchants at Hedeby than anywhere else Haakon might pass on his way home except the Oslofjord. He didn't want to visit there with the treasure still aboard.

King Ethelred ruled Oslofjord with a harsher hand than Haakon thought proper for a ruler of free Norsemen. He also had a reputation for being a little too free with other men's gold.

Ragnar was interested, but wanted to pay only part of Haakon's price for the cargo now. The rest he would pay in the spring, after he was sure of his own profits. Haakon wanted full payment now, and because of his own new wealth, he bargained harder than he might have if he had really been desperate for the money. In the end Ragnar agreed to pay Haakon then and there an amount of silver based on what profit he could reasonably hope to make at Hedeby. He swore a solemn oath before both bands of men that if he made more, he would send Haakon half of the difference before the end of the sailing season next year.

Ragnar was taken with Wulf and offered Haakon a good price for the dog. The offer was firmly refused, but to keep their dealings friendly, Haakon offered Ragnar the pick of the litter if the trader could find a wolfhound bitch to mate with Wulf. Then the two men carved the agreement in runes on sticks of wood and exchanged the sticks.

Haakon's men loaded the walrus tusks, hide ropes, and bales of wadmal aboard Ragnar's *knarr*. Six of Ragnar's men with homes in the Trondelag asked to be paid off and allowed to sail home with Haakon, and both chiefs agreed. Six more men would be welcome aboard Haakon's under-manned ships. Even if they learned something they shouldn't know, they wouldn't be able to talk about it before the treasure was beyond the reach of pirates.

Haakon's ships sailed north from the Frisian coast, across the gray autumn seas, and home to the Trondelag in

Norway. At the mouth of the Trondheimsfjord, they camped
for a day to rest and prepare for the triumphant homecoming. Haakon paid a passing fishing boat's master to take
word ahead that he had won a great victory. He still did
not mention the earl's hoard, even though he no longer
feared pirates or King Ethelred. The Trondelag was a land
under strong law, but men with grandsons able to carry a
spear had still shed blood over less wealth than Haakon
was bringing home.

Haakon came home at noon on a bright, almost windless
day. The rowers in both ships rested on their oars as the
vessels approached the shore, and Haakon scrambled into
Red Hawk's bow. There he was joined by Wulf, who
seemed to understand their journey was at an end. He
danced around Haakon, barking excitedly, then finally
came to rest at his master's feet. As the ship approached
the beach, Haakon stood in the prow with his hand on
Wulf's head.

The ship's beaked head had been long since stowed
away below, to avoid frightening the land spirits. He
braced himself with one arm and cupped the other hand
around his mouth.

"*Harooooo!* We're bringing a great booty from England.
We took an earl's holding and carried off all his gold and
more besides!" He went on, describing the battle and the
courage of some of the men who might have kin among
the crowd on the shore. Shouts, cheers, and war cries
answered him, quickly growing so loud that Haakon gave
up trying to make himself heard. He walked aft and
straddled the boat's side amidships, ready to slip into the
water and wade ashore.

Before Haakon could jump down, a dozen men splashed

out to *Red Hawk*, hoisted him as joyfully as if he had been the most valuable part of the booty, and carried him ashore. Wulf dove into the water and waded to the beach behind the group carrying his master.

It was quite a while before Haakon got his feet on the ground. By the time the first group of men were tired of carrying him up and down the shore like a trophy of victory, more were ready. When Bjorn stepped ashore, he also was lifted into the air. When he pointed out Knut One-Eye and Gunnar as heroes of the battle, still more people ran to carry them. All the freemen joined in, from those who looked too old to carry even their own weight to boys who could barely reach high enough to help. Many of the thralls joined in, and even some of the women.

Haakon had plenty of time to look around at the crowd. His mother, Sigrid Briansdottír, was standing on a little rise of ground. Erik the Bald, a jarl who had been asking for her hand in marriage these past three years, stood nearby. Between them stood old Bosa, an English-born thrall who had risen to be manager of Sigrid's household after twenty years of service to Haakon's father.

Sigrid and Erik seemed to be carefully not looking at each other, while Bosa's gaze kept shifting from one to the other. Haakon wondered if they had quarreled. That thought made him look around for Ivar Egbertsson, Erik's nephew, who usually stayed as close to his uncle as a man's shield to his arm. This was a useful habit, as the nephew had been before the Thing five times for quarrels brought on by his hot temper and easily wounded pride. Erik tried to act as a calming force on his wild kin. Ivar had more than his share of faults, but several times he had listened to Erik's soothing words uttered in the face of Ivar's tempestuous rage. If Sigrid and Erik were angry, Ivar's presence just then would do more harm than good.

By now the pleasure of carrying Haakon's weight around was beginning to wear thin. Haakon was able to stand on his own feet and watch the rest of his men and the booty coming ashore from the ships. He didn't see Ivar or any of his men. It wouldn't be difficult to spot this nephew of Erik's due to the younger man's size. Ivar towered over other oversized Vikings by a head.

Haakon was not truly surprised by Ivar's absence. After all, his steading was two days' travel away. Haakon strode toward his mother.

As they exchanged greetings, he tried to see her as she might look through Erik's eyes. She was still handsome, standing straight and slender, although too dark for most Norse tastes. She set off that darkness well, though, in a rust-red gown of fine wool pinned at her shoulders by massive gold brooches. She held good land as her widow's portion and knew quite well how to manage a home and care for a husband. If she remarried, it would not have to mean trouble for Haakon. He wished his mother would accept Erik, but she rejected any notion of entering a new marriage until her first husband's death had been avenged.

This insistence placed Haakon in a most difficult position. It was because of Sigrid's love and respect for Ole Ketilsson's memory that she harped on Haakon's so-called inability to take action against Olaf Haraldsson, but her nagging not only interfered with their relationship, it also made Haakon doubt his own worth as a son, a warrior, a man.

Haakon and Sigrid had always kept their quarrel inside their steadings. Now that Erik had proposed marriage and had been refused, it was likely to become common knowledge, particularly if Ivar knew about it.

But now Haakon had his golden ax, many followers, much gold and silver, and, best of all, good luck from Thor. He would inform his mother this visit that she and Erik could be married in the spring, if she desired.

He looked at Erik now, and it interested him that the man resembled Ole Ketilsson. The man was not tall but was very broad. His legs were like tree trunks and his forearms were terrifically strong. His receding hair was a strange mixture of blond turning white, and his blue eyes and high cheekbones made Haakon uncomfortable—they were too similar to Ole's.

As it was, Haakon found it hard to say the necessary polite words to Erik. He tried, however, and fortunately the man was in a mood to take them as if they were really meant. Haakon was relieved. It would be casting ill luck on his homecoming to have a public quarrel with Erik, and to avoid that, he uttered a few courtesies proper to the occasion.

Then Erik was gone and Haakon's mother's eyes were aimed at something behind him. Bawdy laughter and shouts came from the shore. He turned to see Rosamund standing amidships aboard *Wave Walker*, looking down at the water. Her hooded cloak concealed her hair, but not her eyes.

Nothing will hide those eyes except death.

Bosa's scarred brown face split into a grin. "More booty, Haakon? For decorating your bed, perhaps?"

Haakon glared with such intensity that Bosa took a step backward, and the jarl was raising a fist when he saw his mother's eyes widen. Sigrid had not only seen the glare, but would remember it. Haakon lowered his hand. Rosamund would be coming into a house Lady Sigrid had considered her domain since her husband's death. Sigrid had her own household, but when Haakon was away, she administered his steading. She was used to being in charge there, and the arrival of Rosamund to take a woman's place in Haakon's home could cause trouble. Two strong women under Haakon's roof would likely quarrel— or keep the peace by making common cause against the man. Neither prospect pleased Haakon.

Bjorn waded out to the ship and held up his arms to Rosamund. She lowered herself onto his shoulders, then clung to his head as he carried her ashore dry-shod. Haakon saw that the mask was back on her face. Looking at his mother, he saw that she wore a similar expression.

XI

Sigrid Briansdottír took her Norse name when she took a Norse husband. A spaewife on Ole Ketilsson's lands said she'd have bad luck if she didn't give up her Irish name. Since she'd already given up her family to marry Ole, her name seemed a rather small thing to give up for good luck in marriage.

It was hard to say whether she'd had luck or not. She had had many good years with Ole, had borne him seven children, had seen four of them live past infancy, and had made peace with her Irish family. Then she saw the quarrel with Olaf Haraldsson blaze up, kill a son and two daughters, strip her husband of his lands, and drive him hurt and grim to die defeated among his kin in the Trondelag.

After that good luck came again. Ole did not fight his last battle in vain, for her husband's kin were willing to let her hold her widow's portion. Her son Haakon became a warrior of note.

Yet her son had not used his war skill to avenge his father. First he was too young and unskilled, then he was himself cursed with bad luck. It seemed that Sigrid's luck had been both good and bad, but always changing. She came to hope that marrying Erik the Bald would end these changes, if and when she consented to be married. But first, Haakon had to fulfill his oath. That was a duty that she now believed her son would never perform. Haakon seemed to have little sense of honor, she surmised, in spite of his promises to sail to Ireland as soon as he had the strength to win a victory there.

Of course Erik could say nothing to interfere. Both he and Sigrid knew this, so there was no need to speak of it and add to Haakon's humiliation. It was not an easy situation for a jarl close to fifty.

Erik hoped Sigrid would consent to the marriage quickly, before the waiting drove him mad. He would have gone mad a year ago if she had not let him share her bed from time to time. It also helped soothe Sigrid's impatience that she was able to rule Haakon's household as if it were her own when he was at sea.

So it was an ugly surprise to Lady Sigrid, when she rode down to her son's steading five days after the homecoming and found Rosamund arranging matters there as if she

were Haakon's wife. An English thrall-girl, in her place!
What happened between the women after that should not
have been a surprise to anyone.

Haakon and Bjorn were walking along a gravel beach. A
small stream flowed across it into the fjord, marking the
boundary between Haakon's own land and his mother's.
From behind them came the thud of a drum and the
ragged chants of hardworking men. Under Snorri's orders
the two crews were hauling *Red Hawk* on rollers into a
ship house for the winter. Beyond the roof of the ship
house, Haakon saw *Wave Walker*'s masthead. She was still
afloat, since there was only room in the ship house for *Red
Hawk*.

"There's enough cut timber to start a new ship house,"
said Haakon. "We should be able to get up the posts and
the roof before the snow comes."

Bjorn looked at the stream. "Do we want to build it so
close to land that—?"

"That may be in Erik's or Ivar's hands next year?"
Haakon knew from the look on Bjorn's face that he'd
spoken more sharply than he intended.

"I suppose that's what I meant."

"My mother hasn't spoken of what she intends to do."

"Neither have you, Haakon."

Haakon knew he should have expected this and should
not be angry. It was hard for him to see the possible
conflict with his own mother as one in which all his
comrades would be guarding his back, as if it were a
regular battle in the field against an armed enemy. Yet, if
any of her land was passed on to Ivar, that sort of conflict
was a possibility.

Haakon took refuge in practical details. "Before we can start pegging timber, we have to find a place with an easier slope. *Wave Walker*'s half again as heavy as *Red Hawk*. We'd find it hard to get her up to the old ship house even if it would hold her."

Before Bjorn could reply, they both heard someone shouting Haakon's name. It was one of his house thralls, who ran up wide-eyed and breathless.

"What is it, Chodric?"

"Lady Sigrid is at the house. She is angry with your English thrall-girl Rosamund. I think they will fight soon."

Haakon spoke his first thought. "The lady Rosamund is not a slave, Chodric. Remember that and tell everyone else. I will beat the next man who calls her a thrall."

Chodric swallowed. "Yes, Haakon."

The boy ran off. Bjorn grabbed Haakon's arm. "Haakon, don't go."

"Why not?"

Bjorn refused to draw back from either Haakon's glare or the iron in his voice. "If you quarrel with your mother over her dealings with Rosamund, what will the people say?"

"They'll say anything they want when I'm out of hearing and be silent in my presence. That's the way it always is. Why should it be otherwise now?"

"Your men have already said she's bewitched you."

"I won't let my mother treat Rosamund as a thrall just to silence tongues that can't be silenced except by cutting them out." He punched Bjorn lightly in the chest. "I know you say this out of fear for me, but don't say it again. I've guarded against my mother's tongue for years. I don't think I've suddenly lost all my skill."

Haakon turned and started up the hillside above the beach. Once he was out of sight of Bjorn he broke into a run. One question thudded in his mind like Snorri's drum.

How long before they come to blows?

He knew the temper his mother had when she was crossed, and now he'd brought into his house a second woman with the same temper. He'd made matters worse by forgetting to give orders either to Rosamund about what she could do or to others about how to treat her.

But something good might come of the day, he realized: He'd been hoping for a chance to speak with his mother about Erik, and he wanted to talk to her before the feast celebrating his homecoming and victory. Erik would certainly be at that feast, probably Ivar as well. Erik would be powerful if he controlled the wealth of Sigrid's holdings in addition to his own. For his part, Ivar could be in a position to inherit those holdings if something befell his uncle. Haakon suspected Ivar was conspiring to gain Sigrid's wealth and lands, but he could not prove it yet. First he must determine just what had gone on during the summer and spring months of his long journey. If, right now, he could turn this approaching confrontation with his mother to that end, then Haakon would know what to expect from Erik, and more particularly, from Ivar. If his mother was too angry to guard her tongue, he might learn all he needed to know.

Haakon slowed to a walk as he came down the hill behind the house. He wanted to arrive with at least enough breath in him to curse both women properly. A number of thralls were standing outside the door, but at least he heard no screams and saw no bodies. He pushed through the thralls and burst into the hall.

Haakon's mother sat in the high seat, her face pale and her hair tangled. Only her quick breathing told Haakon that she was angry. Rosamund stood in front of the older woman, reminding Haakon of a hunting dog facing a bear. Her hair was even more tangled than Sigrid's and one cheek was red. There was a smear of blood on her lower lip, and her gown was ripped along a shoulder.

Haakon looked from one woman to the other. Both looked back at him with the same readiness to let him speak first.

"Rosamund, Lady Sigrid struck you. Why?"

Sigrid began quickly: "She was full of schemes to put this house in—"

"Mother, I was not asking you." If he let his mother use her tongue as freely as she could, he'd be here all day and learn very little.

"I did have *schemes* for doing some work that needs to be done here, Haakon," said Rosamund. "I know that your house is not mine, but I can't keep from putting my hand to work that needs to be done."

"If it needs to be done, then let me do it," said Sigrid. "Don't let it be said that you give an English thrall—"

"*Silence!*"

Haakon was sure the thralls outside the house had heard him. He probably had been heard beyond the bounds of the steading. His mother seemed to shrink back into the high seat, and Haakon saw there was more gray in her hair than he'd remembered. His anger began to fade, but he didn't let this show in his voice.

"Mother, the lady Rosamund is no thrall. Do not call her that again. Rosamund, go on."

Rosamund continued describing the quarrel. It seemed to Haakon that each woman had some right on her side. Sigrid had ruled the house long enough to feel it was her own, but also long enough to grow somewhat careless. Rosamund had seen what had been left undone and had set to work, regardless of how the other woman might feel.

"Rosamund, you say you gave no orders to the house thralls?"

"No. I would not do that without your permission."

"Then you have done nothing wrong. You now have permission to command any thrall in my house. You may go." Rosamund started to kneel, then pulled herself straight and went out. Haakon thought she was trying to keep from smiling.

"What is she to you, Haakon?" said his mother wearily.

"I'll answer that when you tell me what Erik the Bald is to you."

"That has nothing to do with—"

"It has much to do with many things lying between us, Mother. I think it's time we said more about them than we've said the past years. Have you accepted Erik?"

"I haven't said anything this summer I didn't say last year."

"I don't know what you said last year."

"That our marriage is in your hands. What else do you want to know about my relationship with Erik? Why don't you ask me if I'm lying with him?"

Haakon's laugh made his mother stiffen as if he'd slapped her. He realized that he was behaving as if he thought her wits were turned. Whether they were bedding each other or not, if he didn't treat her as a woman of good sense, this quarrel would lead nowhere.

"I'm sorry. You don't need me watching over your virtue."

"Then what are you watching, Haakon? You yourself haven't said much this past year. Am I a witch like—?" She broke off before she could say "Rosamund." "Can I read what's in your heart to use it against you?"

Haakon sighed. His peacemaking gesture seemed to have been wasted. He decided to speak plainly. "What's my fear? Ivar Egbertsson."

"What does he have to do with me?"

"He's been before the Thing three times these past ten years for making claims on other men's lands. He should have been there more often, but he was able to conceal his greed until it was too late for his prey to do anything about it. Is this the sort of man you want as inheritor of your holdings?"

A cold, proud smile. "Haakon, I was able to defend my holdings after your father died. Why should I have trouble with Ivar?"

"You never faced one who was ready to send spearmen against you."

"And Ivar will?"

"Can you say he won't?"

"I can say he won't if his uncle opposes it."

"Will his uncle do so?"

"Erik will, if I accept him."

"I see." Sigrid's assurance was no guaranty of either man's behavior. It certainly didn't mean Erik could be trusted to stand against his nephew Ivar.

"I am not sure you do. Erik has also said he would have to take my refusing him as an insult from you. I told him this was not correct reasoning. You can understand why I have told Erik that only when I am a free woman, will I accept him."

"But only as long as you don't accept Ivar as well—"

"Could you say that more clearly?"

She had the right to ask, although it would have been much easier to explain if there had been more good will on both sides. As it was, he had to sound as if he were laying down the law, avoiding anything she might hear as weakness.

Ivar Egbertsson was not a neighbor Haakon liked or one he wanted to see get too close or too powerful. Haakon told Sigrid that Ivar might become both if Sigrid married Erik the Bald.

"Ivar may covet other people's property, but he's never done it in my presence."

"Perhaps. But what if you die? You'll not see forty again, Mother."

"No, although Erik does his best to make me forget it." She smiled.

Haakon was quite sure now that Erik was bedding her, and equally sure it was none of his concern. She'd been alone for too many years. He sighed. Everything would have been so much easier if he could have just forced himself to be utterly brutal with his mother. But he could have done so only if his own conscience were entirely clear over not yet avenging his father. As it was, he fought with a blunted sword when he fought with his mother.

"No one can know his wyrd or escape it," he said. "You may outlive us all, but what if you don't? Do you want me

and my sons to have to sleep spear-in-hand because Ivar
Egbertsson's lands run too close to ours?"

"If you think that could come . . ."

"It could."

"I do not see it as you do," she replied. "But since you
see danger, what do you ask from me to guard against it?"

"His public oath that if you die before he does, your
lands come back to me."

"I will not ask him that."

"Then I will. If he wants to make a quarrel out of the
matter, the sooner it comes into the open air, the better
for us all."

"Are you going to push him into the quarrel?"

"That is not in my hands." Haakon would swear nothing
to his mother now. If Erik the Bald would swear before
the Thing to return Sigrid's lands, he could marry her
with Haakon's blessing and a fistful of English silver to pay
for the wedding feast. That would win enough safety
against Ivar's schemes without shaming his mother or
letting the whole Trondelag know of their quarrel.

"And Ivar?"

"I'll spend the winter choosing spearmen for my voyaging next summer. If Ivar tries anything, I'll be able to give
him the sort of answer he respects."

They talked a while longer, about the crops, the thralls,
and other safe matters, but they didn't part with smiles.
When Sigrid left, Haakon's only consolation was that
Rosamund's name hadn't been mentioned once after she
had gone. At least there might be fewer tongues than
Bjorn had feared wagging about "Haakon's quarrel with
Lady Sigrid over the English witch-girl"; he was certain
his mother would not tell tales about their discussion.

XII

It seemed to the people in Haakon's house that Lady Sigrid retreated to her own steading without challenging her son to a battle over Rosamund. As a result, Haakon felt free to give the younger woman charge of his household. Some people still grumbled, saying that even if Rosamund was not a thrall, she was still no woman to give orders to free Norsemen. Rosamund's tongue silenced some of the grumblers and Haakon's fists subdued most of the others. Within a few days the matter was settled, at least to Haakon's satisfaction. The work of preparing the feast went forward.

Rosamund was less satisfied—when she had time to think about anything except the work, which kept her busy from dawn until sunset and sometimes well into the night. Her plan of becoming indispensable to Haakon seemed to be working, at least as far as menial labor was concerned. But Haakon seldom came to her bed even when he spent the night at home; and when he did, even less often did he turn to her for more than physical warmth. She suspected that it was only the festering quarrel involving his mother that kept him so aloof. She knew that if this was so, there was little she could do to ease him.

She told herself that Haakon was honorable, that she

was in no danger, and indeed that she had been only a little less alone in her own father's house. All of this was true and even made her wonder if she could find it in herself to love her captor. Yet none of it made her bed any warmer as the nights grew longer.

She did what she could. She asked questions where she dared, and where she didn't, she listened carefully. After a few days the men and women of the house were speaking freely in her presence.

Bjorn had more time to grow fretful. "There's no more talk of her witchcraft now," he told Haakon one night. "But will you wager that matters stay peaceful until sailing time in the spring?"

"*Wave Walker's* men won't leave over some quarrel in my house. If some of ours do, we'll have younger sons from all over the Trondelag at the feast. We can find men to fill the empty benches before the snow gets deep; let it all alone until spring."

"What if we can't get enough men?"

"Then we don't sail in the spring. We may be staying home then anyway—until we've made a sure peace with Erik and Ivar." He gripped Bjorn by both shoulders. "Old friend, what is there about Rosamund that is eating at you this way? Do you suspect she's a witch? I swear I will be angry with you unless you tell the truth now!"

"She's laid no spells on you that any fair woman couldn't," Bjorn said slowly. "She knows more than enough about ruling a household. But—Haakon, I'm not Gunnar. My words don't come easily. But . . . I wish I knew whose voice you hear when Rosamund speaks to you."

Bjorn expected laughter, anger, or at least a demand

that he explain. He hadn't expected Haakon to look as if he'd been struck in the face.

"Whose voice do you think I hear? When Rosamund speaks, I hear her voice. Then I hear my own in response. I am not bewitched, Bjorn."

"You are different, Haakon. I have noticed it, the other men have seen it. This is not the way to keep the men by your side. There is much talk."

Haakon shook his head, feeling sorry for Bjorn's inability to understand. But Bjorn had never had a woman in the same sense that Haakon had Rosamund.

"I have changed only because my luck has changed. In the past, I worried only about keeping my men fed and my ships in repair. Now I have greater concerns." They came upon a large boulder. Haakon sat down and motioned his old friend to join him.

"Bjorn, I will tell you true. Rosamund is my prisoner. We could ask a large ransom from Earl Edmund for her safe return. But I cannot make myself take the steps toward such an act. I ask myself: Haakon, is it because you are depriving Harud Olafsson of his bride and therefore Olaf Haraldsson, as well? Or is there something about Lady Rosamund herself that you must keep for yourself? I do not know. I have been staying away from her just to clear my thoughts. I know when I am not with her, I think of her."

Bjorn nodded. Although he did not fully understand him, Bjorn was satisfied to know that Haakon was at least trying to determine a path for himself rather than allowing Rosamund to decide it for him. As long as Haakon was still in control, that was all that mattered to the helmsman.

"I will do my part to help you. I will tell the men."

Haakon heaved himself to his feet, then offered his hand to his friend. Once Bjorn was standing, Haakon walked away, slowly shaking his head.

The hall was dark, and the air was thick with woodsmoke; it smelled of damp fur, mead, burned meat, and vomit. The victory feast had gone as well as planned—no, better. The snores and groans of restless sleepers on the floor, on the benches, and in the sleeping chambers on either side sounded like a distant storm. Normally Rosamund could find her way about the house blindfolded and even ignore such smells. Tonight she was stumbling over sleeping bodies or empty bowls, and the air made her gag if she took a deep breath.

Much of her revulsion was her own fault. How much had she drunk anyway? Enough so that her feet would not always go where she wanted them. There had been mead and good ale and even some German wine, and Haakon's grim face made her drink more every time she looked at him. She didn't look too often, afraid he would notice how uneasy she was.

She had begun to think there was something else besides the quarrel with his mother, something eating at him from within like a canker. Now he slept restlessly nearby.

Suddenly she knew she had to breathe fresh air. She stumbled toward the door, somehow reached it without waking anyone, and staggered up the stairs to the grass outside. The cold night air burned her lungs, and for a moment she went down on her hands and knees, afraid she was going to vomit. After a few deep breaths the burning died away, her churning stomach quieted, and she was able to stand.

There was just enough moonlight to silver the frosty grass. She saw a shadow stretching toward her across the silver. At the end of that shadow stood a patch of deeper darkness. She pulled her cloak tighter about her and waited, without knowing quite what she was waiting for.

"Lady Rosamund." She didn't recognize the voice.

"Yes?"

"I am Ivar Egbertsson and I would like to speak with you alone."

Ivar Egbertsson, Erik's nephew, no friend to Haakon, but someone who might be useful, if not trustworthy. Rosamund fought down a laugh rising in her throat. Her father had very much the same reputation as Ivar. After years of dealing with him, Ivar would be child's play.

She realized with a start that the drink in her was drowning out the voice of caution. If Ivar had sought her out here and now for secret words, he probably meant Haakon no good. Had he shouted this thought in her ear, she could not have been more certain. She knew she was facing a man prepared to betray his host and neighbor, dishonor his house and men. What was there to keep him from killing her the moment he thought she might be dangerous to him? Neither thrall nor free, a Christian, an Englishwoman, she had no one here to protect her except Haakon, and would he think she was worth it?

Suddenly her thoughts at least were almost sober. "I'll come with you, as long as you swear you mean nothing against my life or honor."

"By Odin, Thor, and my own hope of a good death, I mean you no harm," said Ivar.

"Very well."

It was colder than she'd realized at first. By the time

she'd followed the man to a sheltered corner behind the brewhouse, she was fighting hard not to shiver. She did not want him to even suspect she was afraid.

"Do you mean any harm to Haakon?" was her first question. The answer was silence, except for the wind. Apparently he had expected her to listen first, then speak afterward, if at all. For a moment anger warmed her, though she knew that anger could put her in even more danger than fear. First her father and brothers, then Haakon, now this man, each seemed to expect her to stay in her place, to wait like a peg on a wall for whatever he chose to hang on her for his own pleasure, in his own good time.

"Do you?" she repeated.

Ivar cleared his throat. "I can't swear peace with Haakon when he cares so little for peace with me. I'll say that I mean him no harm unless he strikes at me. Why do you ask, Lady Rosamund? Have you sworn to guard his back, after what he's done to you?"

"I've sworn no such oath. But I know that for now, Haakon's safety is mine. His house is my only refuge here in the Norse lands. Why should I be such a fool as to put myself in danger?"

"But no oath?"

"No, and I won't swear one to you, either." She would not pit herself against Haakon unless he treated her cruelly, and so far he had done nothing worse than turn coldly indifferent. The devil you know is better than the devil you don't. She drew her cloak tightly about her again, although for all the warmth she felt, it might have been made of straw. "I won't stand here in the wind listening to empty words, either."

"I ask no oath," said Ivar. "I only ask you to think of me as a man who can help you see England again."

"At what price?"

There ensued a long silence. Rosamund sensed that this man wished to be elsewhere and dared not say much for fear of telling Rosamund something she shouldn't know. A desire to laugh joined her fear and anger. So what if she only had a part of Haakon? Half of him was worth as much as the whole of this fool.

"I want to go home," she said. "What do you want me to do?"

"Speak for me to Haakon," said Ivar. "My uncle wants to marry Lady Sigrid. I don't want a quarrel with Haakon. "If you can make him understand that we mean him no harm by the marriage to his mother, I shall be grateful."

If she had heard any affection for Sigrid in Ivar's words, Rosamund would have felt sorry for him. As it was, his words rang unpleasantly false. But even if she were wrong and he were honest, he certainly wanted more than that from her. Ivar might grow suspicious if she pressed matters further, though. He might also take her for a fool if she didn't, and that would be only a little less dangerous.

"What else do you want?" She had to fight not to hold her breath.

"I want you to watch Haakon gathering his men and ships for next spring," said Ivar. "Learn how many men he swears to his service, what weapons he gives them, what he does with *Wave Walker*."

"You fear an attack from Haakon?"

"It's one way of keeping Sigrid from marrying Erik," said Ivar. "He was angry when my uncle wouldn't swear to let her lands return to him if Erik outlived her."

Rosamund swallowed her surprise as well as her anger at learning something so important from Haakon's enemy first and not from him. She frowned and dropped her cloak. "Is that enough reason for war?"

"For Haakon Olesson it could be."

"Would the Thing say so?"

"I don't know. A man like Haakon can pay a witness to swear for him. If he uses his gold even more freely, he could find enough spearmen to strike us down before anyone could ask questions. You understand that we would like to be warned if he is gathering such a band."

"And if I spy for you, you'll take me home?"

"As soon as we can."

"I wish I could promise all you want, but—"

"Why not?" Ivar sounded angry.

"Because I don't know as much about Haakon's affairs as you may think, and I won't have any information before spring." That wasn't quite as much of a lie as she'd thought she'd have to tell, but she still hoped Ivar wouldn't ask her to explain.

"But—in the spring?"

"Who knows? If I find myself where I can help you, I'll do it. As for speaking to Haakon about Erik and Sigrid, I can do that now. How much you think that help is worth is for you to decide."

Ivar still hadn't answered that question when she heard the crunching of boots on frost-crisped grass and found herself alone. Her cloak lay on the ground and the wind blew even colder. She started to pick up the cloak, then stopped with it trailing on the ground as a thought struck her as abruptly as an arrow.

He'd gone away and left her, perhaps satisfied with their

agreement. Rosamund felt a warmth flow through her,
from her throat down to her toes and was glad no one
could see her in this darkness. If she could follow Ivar and
learn more about his scheme, then she might have something worth telling Haakon, something to give him a real
weapon against his enemies. Ivar might meet with another
man to tell him of her response. Maybe Erik was partner
to this scheme. Rosamund loosened her knife in its sheath
on her belt, wrapped her cloak around her, and began
stalking Ivar in the dark.

XIII

The buildings of Haakon's steading were scattered wide-
ly. Rosamund found it easy to keep the man in sight, but
she also had to take great care that he didn't see her
following him. He probably wouldn't risk awakening the
steading by trying to kill her—since he had told her
practically nothing about his real plans—nonetheless, she
didn't want to destroy her chances of learning those plans.

She slipped from one pool of shadow to another. The
frost bit through the soles of her shoes until her toes
stiffened, and the wind searched out every opening in her
gown. The wind and the stampings of horses and cattle in
the sheds were the only sounds she didn't make herself. It
was a night when ghosts might walk more readily than
men, when the clouds race fearfully past the moon.

Rosamund would have given a good deal to have Wulf at

her heels. She hadn't thought she would need him when she left the house. By now he was probably asleep in Haakon's chamber. Waking him would mean waking his new master. For once she felt angry at Wulf for his change of allegiance.

Ivar seemed headed for the western edge of the steading, where there were more trees than buildings. Here a good many of the guests at the feast were spending the night, including Lady Sigrid and her people. Rosamund saw him stop in the shadow of a young oak, with a shed beyond it. Then the moon slipped behind a blanket of clouds and the whole world was suddenly in darkness. Rosamund pulled her cloak over her face and ran light-footed into the shed. From just inside its door she could hear Ivar clearly with little danger of being discovered. Apparently Ivar Egbertsson had been met by an accomplice, for she overheard a report of her conversation.

"She won't cause trouble. She seemed willing enough to return to England."

"Then I will come back in the spring after I have prepared my men and the ice has broken. When Rosamund is delivered, you will be well paid in gold, enough to take Sigrid's and Haakon's lands."

Mark! Rosamund sank back onto the wall of the shed. Her heart was pounding in her ears and she could barely catch her breath. What was her brother doing here? It was obvious to Rosamund, once she could think clearly, that Mark had come to rescue her from Haakon and possibly to then deliver her to Harud.

Her first impulse was to rush outside, fall into her brother's arms, and cry, "No! I will not go! I will remain with this man Haakon." But then she realized that if she showed herself now, there would be nothing to prevent Mark from taking her back to England with him this very night.

She had to get away from this place quickly. She was not willing to pay the heavy price of an unplanned reunion with her brother.

Rosamund leaned heavily against the rough timber of the shed wall. She knew she had to quickly tell someone about Ivar asking her to spy for him, even more quickly than she'd planned. If she tried to work alone even for a few days, Haakon would lose the advantage of time. If Mark was planning to return to the Trondelag, he might well be planning to bring Harud Olafsson with him—and perhaps Earl Edmund and Olaf Haraldsson.

As far as Rosamund could tell, Erik was not party to this treachery. Mark could have come here, quickly sought out the names of Haakon's enemies, and enlisted Ivar Egbertsson without Erik the Bald ever knowing of the scheme. The only person who could determine Erik's innocence, or lack thereof, would be Sigrid herself.

If Rosamund told Haakon of what she had learned, he might assume Erik's involvement and part of his temper might be turned against his mother. The uneasy peace between Haakon and Sigrid could fall apart. Ivar might be tempted into open warfare at a time when he could easily be stronger and better prepared than Haakon. Rosamund also did not particularly want to add to Lady Sigrid's burdens. The woman had done a good deal that was wrong, but nothing to deserve her spending her last years in disgrace.

Suddenly Rosamund felt a warm excitement flowing

through her. If she told Lady Sigrid what had passed tonight, would Sigrid listen? Perhaps she would not believe it all, coming from someone she thought was an enemy. But she could not be enough of a fool to ignore it completely. And she would be ready when Erik came, able to ask questions the man might not be able to answer easily. Whatever happened after that could hardly do much good for Erik and Ivar or much harm to Haakon and Sigrid.

Of course, all this depended on Sigrid's not killing her outright and not being a fool. Against outright murder Rosamund could defend herself as she had against Ivar, by a threat to rouse the whole steading. She also did not think Lady Sigrid was the kind of fool who could not count fingers held up in front of her face. Some of the men around the steading did call her foolish, and even Haakon sometimes doubted her, but Rosamund did not let this bother her. Most men were very unreliable witnesses to a woman's wisdom.

Again Rosamund made sure of her knife. Then she stood up and walked briskly across the grass toward the guest-house where Sigrid lay.

Sigrid Briansdottír woke from dreams she could never remember afterward, because what she saw when she awoke drove all memories out of her. She saw Haakon's English bed-girl, Rosamund, standing over her sleeping pallet, looking as if she were not quite of this world. Around the two women echoed the snores and the mutterings of the restless sleepers among Sigrid's household. Sigrid saw no one awake and able to help her against Rosamund.

She's slipped into the house like a thief, and there's nothing and no one to keep her from killing me—

"Lady Sigrid, I would like to speak with you alone." Sigrid sat up, clutching her robe and furs around her, and opened her mouth to shout. Swiftly Rosamund knelt beside her, one hand on her wrist and the other a finger's breadth from her mouth. "No. What I have to say concerns only you and me, and in time Haakon. I swear you are in no danger from me."

Sigrid fought back an urge to bite the hand near her mouth, then stiffened as Rosamund drew her knife. "Lady Sigrid, you do not trust me. Very well, I give you my knife. I will stand before you unarmed while I speak if you will come with me and listen to what I have to say."

Sigrid wanted to make a gesture to ward off evil spirits, then to scream with all her breath. Rosamund's so nearly reading her thoughts hadn't made her any more willing to go out into the cold alone with the girl. On the other hand, she would *not* give her son's bedmate a chance to doubt her courage.

"Very well." Sigrid took the knife and held it while she wrapped herself up as well as she could one-handed. Then she followed Rosamund out of the hut, keeping her at a distance so the girl would have no chance to snatch the knife back.

The night was colder than Sigrid had expected, and it seemed to grow colder as Rosamund told her tale. Before long Sigrid knew why Rosamund had brought her out here, where no one could hear. It was ugly enough to hear as it was. If the rest of her household knew, or her son . . . Sigrid began to feel as if she'd swallowed a large stone, while a band of iron was tightening around her neck.

It would have been easier if she could have screamed at Rosamund, "You whore! You're lying and I know it!" She couldn't. If she *knew* anything, it was that Rosamund was telling the truth. At least she was telling the truth about Ivar and Mark, and had honestly stated her uncertainty about Erik's part.

Sigrid was no longer hearing Rosamund's voice. She felt her legs quivering, and the stone in her stomach grew so large she wanted to vomit. Then Rosamund had an arm around her shoulders and was leading her somewhere, as if she'd been a child. In a little while there was a warmer darkness all around them, smelling of hay and animals. She felt straw under her feet and heard the lowing of the milk cows.

"Are you sick, Lady Sigrid? I think there's enough fire left to heat some milk and—"

"No, no. I'm—" Words wouldn't come. Sigrid waved her hands in front of her face as if she wanted to drive away stinging flies. Then she ran her fingers through her hair, wincing as she caught knots and tangles. She looked Rosamund in the face.

"Rosamund, why didn't you accept Ivar's bargain? And if you weren't going to accept it, why did you come to me and not to Haakon?" She gripped a fistful of straw in each hand. "If I understand this . . ."

Rosamund swallowed. "I refused him because I know the kind of man he is. He wouldn't keep a promise to the Mother of God herself!" Her voice fell to a whisper. "My father is too much like him. I would gain nothing, plus give him a weapon he could thrust into me any time he wanted."

She took a deep breath. "Another reason goes beyond a likeness to my father—to a resemblance to the devil himself. I was betrothed. The ceremony was to have been observed the week after Haakon besieged the castle. My betrothed is a man of evil, and he learned that from his father. I would have been at both their mercies—Harud Olafsson and Olaf Haraldsson alike. I feared for my li—"

Rosamund abruptly ended her explanation as Lady Sigrid swooned, her eyes rolling back in her head and her jaw dropping wide.

"Sigrid! My lady!" Rosamund ran out into the cold in panic looking for help, then seeing no one, back into the barn. She dragged Sigrid to a watering trough in the next stall and immersed her hands and wrists in the frigid water. She patted some on the woman's cheeks until signs of consciousness returned.

After several minutes, it became Sigrid's turn to explain. A deep bond developed between the two women, fixed permanently by an intense hatred of a common enemy. Their fates were obviously intertwined. Sigrid took Rosamund's hand and looked searchingly into the purple-blue eyes.

"Do you love Haakon?"

Sigrid had the small victory of seeing Rosamund speechless for a moment. Then the younger woman closed her eyes. "I think I—no, I don't have the words for it. Perhaps I do. It doesn't matter. What does matter is that my life is in Haakon's hands. Why should I do anything to weaken him? I'd have been doing that if I had made the quarrel between you and him any worse. If I'd spoken to him instead of you—"

Sigrid had stopped listening. In spite of Rosamund's own doubts, she knew how matters stood with the girl and Haakon. Rosamund loved him desperately, and it was hard to believe that if he saw this, he wouldn't respond. A woman worthy of him had finally come to Haakon. Sigrid had known for years this might happen.

The stone in Sigrid's stomach melted so suddenly that she was sobbing desperately before she realized it. She tried to control herself, weeping like this in front of Rosamund, but failed. She bent forward, throwing her hair over her face, vaguely aware of Rosamund's arms around her, but suddenly clearly aware of the sounds of approaching footsteps.

Sigrid jumped up, obviously about to scream. Rosamund fell backwards and stared at the doorway. Then they both heard a familiar voice.

"What's going on here, if you please?"

It was Bjorn, bare chested, barefooted, and with a naked sword in his hand. He was swaying rather like a pine tree in the breeze. Rosamund stared at him, desperately whipping her thoughts to move faster than they ever had before. Telling the truth would expose the night's doing to a man who didn't like her and might not trust Lady Sigrid. A lie might not be discovered, but on the other hand, if it was, matters would certainly be worse than before. Also, people said Bjorn was unhappy about Haakon's not trusting him as fully in the quarrel with Sigrid as he was trusted in other matters. If Rosamund proved that she at least trusted him, it might help make peace between them.

Rosamund helped Lady Sigrid sit down again, then told Bjorn everything that had happened since she left the hall. Although he was leaning against the wall of the barn by the time she'd finished, he had heard her out without interruption.

Bjorn snorted. Then he realized that both women were staring at him, waiting to hear what he would say to Rosamund's story. He sighed and shook his head slowly.

"Rosamund, Lady Sigrid. I don't know what to make of this. Fortunately it isn't for me to make anything of it. It's for Haakon to do that." A faint smile. "But I'll see that he does it, I promise you."

"You think I'm telling the truth?" said Rosamund.

"Yes. I have known Ivar and Erik a long time." Lady Sigrid winced at the implied reproach. Rosamund stepped closer to her, torn between relief and a desire to snarl at Bjorn for his ill-timed words.

Bjorn propped his sword against the wall and pressed both hands against his forehead. "I'll send for some men to watch Erik and Ivar. Rosamund, you take Lady Sigrid—"

"No," said Rosamund. She found herself beginning to sway on her feet, but her thoughts were still coming. "If we start watching Erik and Ivar now, they'll know something's wrong. Ivar might start a fight at once, before Haakon's new men are ready. And we do not want to assume Erik's guilt." She hoped she hadn't broken the fragile truce between herself and Bjorn by practically giving him an order.

He nodded. "That's true enough. Then I'll continue repairing Haakon's ships and building the fighting forces.

That shouldn't tell those swine anything. They'll believe we're preparing for the spring sailing to Ireland, which is no secret around here. Haakon has been planning to find Olaf Haraldsson anyway. If we have the chance to fight him on our turf, so much the better."

"And I will do my share by testing Erik's position on this matter. If he is involved, then he will find his due rewards. If he is innocent, then he will have a wife," Sigrid said.

When Rosamund returned from putting Lady Sigrid to bed, Haakon was still sound asleep under a double mound of furs. Bjorn was also asleep just outside his chief's door.

Inside the chamber, Rosamund stripped off her own clothes and crawled in under the furs beside him. Fortunately he was lying in a position that let her curl up against him. She'd discovered that no matter how tired you were, it was easier to get to sleep on a cold night if there was a warm body in the bed with you.

XIV

Haakon woke up with a dry mouth and a thunderstorm in his head. He hadn't thought he'd drunk enough to make his head hurt this much.

"Rosamund!" What he'd intended as a roar came out as a croak. What had he done last night besides drink too much? He groaned at the pain in his head. Then Rosamund was there beside the bed.

"How was the feast? I barely remember it," he managed to say. Rosamund only held a cup of hot ale to his lips. He smelled herbs in the steam, drank deeply, then repeated his question.

"You were a gracious and generous host. You encouraged your guests to take full advantage of the food and drink, as you yourself did. Then you fell unceremoniously forward on the table. Bjorn and I put you to bed. Can you see me clearly?" Haakon blinked, then nodded. "Good. The best thing for you to do is go back to sleep."

Haakon had the vague feeling she was trying to keep something from him and a strong feeling that he had to empty his bladder. By the time he'd done that, he knew he wasn't strong enough to ask any questions right now, even if Rosamund was lying. He was asleep again a moment after Rosamund piled the furs over him.

The next time Haakon awoke, Rosamund was already sitting on a stool beside the bed. A chill in the air suggested that it was evening. His head still ached, but he was more thirsty than anything else. While he emptied a jug of water, the door opened and Lady Sigrid and Bjorn came in.

A look Haakon didn't understand passed between his mother and Rosamund. "They're gone?" the girl asked.

"A good mile on their way at sunset," said Bjorn. "And there's no one outside the door except Gunnar and Knut."

Haakon made a noise like a hungry bear and started to sit up. Immediately he learned that he still wasn't strong enough to sit up if both Bjorn and Rosamund were pushing him back down into the bed.

Then his mother stepped up to the foot of the bed and quietly began to tell him everything that had happened last night. She didn't weep or kneel, although by the time she'd finished she looked as if she would have felt better if she could. Instead she stood straighter than before and waited for her son's reply.

Haakon knew he shouldn't make her wait. It would surely seem cruel, and it might shatter the fragile peace she was offering. He still found it hard to believe that what he'd heard was actually what she'd said.

Yet—he wasn't drunk, and he doubted that last night's ale and mead were making him hear imaginary things.

What are you waiting for? A sign from Thor that you should believe your own mother?

The voice was in Haakon's mind, but it sounded so much like Bjorn that he was glaring at the man before realizing that nothing had been said. Haakon sat up, and this time no one tried to keep him down.

"Are you saying that you'll give up Erik?"

Sigrid shook her head. "I'll give him a chance to explain himself. I will ask him to swear to let my land come back to you if I die before he does. I will also ask him to swear peace with you before the Thing. If he does all this, I will at least not refuse to see him."

She sighed. "Haakon, I won't say that everything I've done through wanting to marry Erik was foolish. I do not see him as a man who might be dangerous to you. He may prove a valuable ally against Ivar's treachery. Haakon, I will not place you or Rosamund in danger, but I must know if there is a stain in Erik's heart."

"Mother, you don't need to beg. I have not said and done everything for the best—at least during this past year. I told the truth when I said I would sail to Ireland when I had enough men and ships and our affairs here were in good order. If we all stand together now, our enemies can do nothing."

"They aren't beaten yet," said Bjorn.

"I'm not burying them yet," replied Haakon sharply. "I do say that a man with gold, spearmen, and no need to guard his back from his own kin is a match for most enemies. We should be able to settle with Ivar, Mark, Olafsson, and even Haraldsson one way or another before high summer."

No one seemed to have anything more to say after that. Rosamund finally broke the silence by leading Sigrid and Bjorn out, then returning to crawl under the furs beside Haakon. He kissed her and put an arm around her, squeezing her breasts and wishing he could do much more to show his gratitude for all she'd done. His head was beginning to throb again, though. He might not be able to summon the strength to perform vigorously if he tried to take her now.

Her warmth beside him and her even breathing in his ear were lulling him to sleep. He sighed contentedly and slid deeper under the furs. It seemed that the two strong women under his roof had indeed united, but his enemies had far more to fear from this than he did.

Restoring peace to his household did not solve any of Haakon's problems with his enemies. The moment he was able to get out of bed, Haakon returned to the work he'd begun the night of the feast, learning who among the men of the Trondelag would follow him. He didn't deny that his men might need to follow him into battle against Ivar and Mark, although he knew this would probably cost him some oaths. Anyone worth having with him would know the truth, and lying would be an insult to such men. He would rather have fewer men, those he could trust, than have any who might not be reliable.

Haakon called Rosamund, Sigrid, and Bjorn together a few days later and described his work.

"We are well on the road to being strong enough by spring to fight and win. By summer we could be so strong that even Ivar and Mark may choose peace. For now, however, we do not have enough men we can trust in the sort of fight we may face this winter.

"So we have to be careful that Ivar does not learn how much matters have changed in this house. If he does, he may be tempted to strike quickly, while he knows he has the advantage." All knew that Haakon was thinking of his father, who'd lost land, son, daughters, and, in time, life to an enemy who struck quickly.

"I'm not going to lie with Erik again merely to help keep this secret," said Lady Sigrid sharply. He had refused to swear the oaths she had asked of him; however, he'd left before harsh words passed between them.

"I wasn't asking that," said Haakon.

"Good. I am mistress of my own bed, and Erik is no longer welcome in it. I could not determine either his innocence or guilt in Ivar's scheme. I only know that he is unwilling to take my side in this matter of my land. He refuses to believe any unkind words about his nephew. I was not able to say all I felt about Ivar without revealing how much we know; but as far as I am concerned, my request for the lands should be enough for him. Until Erik decides that my wishes should prevail over his loyalty to his nephew, our wedding is canceled."

Rosamund leaned over and took Sigrid's hand.

Haakon sighed. Peace hadn't blunted his mother's tongue. He'd probably be arguing with her as often as before, if not as harshly.

"Lady Sigrid," said Bjorn. "What do you say to this: Tell Erik that Haakon mutters threats against him, that he may even lie in wait for Erik some night, to see that he never returns home. This threat might force Erik to display his true nature."

Sigrid shook her head. "He would protect himself in any event. We would learn nothing we don't already know. Erik is no coward."

"I didn't say he was," said Bjorn. "But any man will think carefully before traveling in a Trondelag winter if he knows he has enemies wanting his blood."

The others nodded. In the winter a man's disappearance could always be blamed on wolves or foul weather. By spring no one would be able to prove otherwise, even if the body did come to light.

"Erik might not be a coward," said Rosamund. "But I think we all can see that a threat will prove nothing and may create new problems. He may be driven to join his nephew if he believes Haakon is an enemy. No, I am afraid we will only learn Erik's true thoughts next spring, when the fighting begins."

Haakon and Sigrid nodded. It occurred to Haakon that Bjorn might say he was hiding behind a woman's skirts with this approach. Bjorn meant him no harm. It was just difficult for the older man to trust the mind of a woman.

As for Haakon trusting Rosamund—well, he would watch her if that made Bjorn happier. He trusted her so completely, however, that he did not know whether this trust was something else coming from Valhalla, or whether it was coming from what now lay between him and Rosamund. He did know that the trust was there, and he did not expect Rosamund to do anything to make it go away.

Snow lay heavy in the Trondelag that winter, but the cold was less bitter than usual. Some days were so fine that a skilled sailor could take a boat along the shore or even across the Trondheimsfjord.

Lady Sigrid stayed close to her steading but sent news and good wishes to her son and Rosamund every few days. She reported that Erik the Bald had grumbled somewhat when she had told him to spend the winter at home, but he did seem to be following either her wishes or Ivar's in the matter. Certainly she didn't see him after the snows came.

From Ivar Egbertsson's replies to Rosamund's inaccurate "spy" messages, it seemed that he also was staying close to home this winter, keeping himself warm with ale and thrall-girls.

Other men had reasons to wrap themselves in fur and wool, pull on boots, pick up staffs, and struggle through the snow. Snorri Longfoot went down to the shore practically every day. At first it was to finish the second ship house and get *Wave Walker* pulled up inside it. Then it was to push along the work of both ships.

Haakon made frequent, regular rounds between the house, the ships, and the huts where some of his men were passing the winter. He'd sworn more than forty new men to his service before the snows came. Half of them were wintering on their own steadings, and he could only hope their weapons and oaths would prove good in the spring. The others were his guests, and he could make

sure that they sharpened their spears and swords, repaired
their armor, stayed sober most of the time, and got outside
for weapons practice whenever the weather would permit.

Bjorn was Haakon's good right hand whenever something needed doing and his chief couldn't be there. He
saw the new spearmen turning into fighters he'd be happy
to lead in battle, although they still kept a little apart from
the men who'd fought under Haakon last summer. He saw
Gunnar singing most of his songs into Guthrun's ear, and
the maid was intently listening. He saw Knut the One-Eye
turning into a leader so readily followed that Bjorn was
happier than ever that they could be sure of the man's
loyalty.

Rosamund, with Wulf at her heels, kept the steading in
better order than anyone under forty could remember it
having been. On fine days they would play in the snow
until Wulf was white as an Iceland bear and Rosamund's
cheeks were apple-red from the cold. Then she'd run back
inside and huddle close to the hearth fires, or close to
Haakon under the furs in their bed.

Huddling close to Haakon always ended one way, and
she was now as eager as he, sometimes more so after he'd
spent a long day working on the ships. She had the feeling
from their lovemaking that they were drinking special
wine, the last and sweetest mouthful, which filled them
with a new and delicious sort of drunkenness. She also
knew that the only way to keep this sensation was to grip
Haakon even more closely.

Wulf began the winter by sleeping in Haakon's chamber, at the foot of the bed. This ended one night when he
awoke, thought Haakon was attacking his lady, and bit
Haakon on the buttocks at the most embarrassing possible

moment. After that Haakon did not sit comfortably for several days, and Wulf had to find his own sleeping place and his own company.

Rosamund was not breeding by the end of the winter and found this preying on her spirits. Haakon consoled her. "First, you're young. Second, I don't expect to become a monk. Third, if Ivar or Mark learned you were carrying my child, they might wonder where your loyalties were. Then both you and the child would be in danger."

Rosamund heard the words without accepting them or stopping her prayers for a child. She hadn't been within ten days' journey of a priest since she reached the Trondelag, so she wasn't sure to whom she prayed or who might answer her prayers. She could only hope they would be answered. With a child of Haakon's in her, no one could doubt where her loyalty stood.

XV

Spring came, with dripping gray skies and mud everywhere. Then the skies turned blue and the mud dried. The spearmen who'd spent the winter on their own lands came to Haakon's steading. He now had more than ninety men following him, and he put them to work.

In the morning they ran, jumped, heaved rocks, and wrestled until they'd worked up a good sweat. Then the day's real work began. They threw spears and shot arrows at targets on trees and in the sand. They fought as two shield walls and charged toward each other with clubs, trying to break each other's lines. When they'd finished all this, they did it again. As the day drew to a close, they raced down to the shore and plunged into the fjord, with Haakon leading them.

They did this day after day, in the woods, in the high meadows, and on the beaches. Haakon asked as much of himself as he asked of his men, and often more. Even so, some men grumbled and three went home. Haakon let them go and ignored the grumbling. The complaints grew less as the men gained skill and began to take pride in being stronger and faster than ever before. They began to call themselves Dark Haakon's Iron Band, although Bjorn said it was unlucky for men to take such a name before they'd proved themselves in battle.

"Half of them already have proved themselves," Haakon reminded him. "As for the others, anything that makes them fight better won't hurt us."

"No," said Bjorn. They both knew that fighting a neighbor could spell dangers not faced when raiding the English or the Franks. Their ninety men could deal with Ivar and Mark alone, but would be hard-pressed if Erik and his men were Ivar's allies. With luck Ivar would find no one willing to take his side in this quarrel, but they could hardly gamble their victory on that.

It was getting on toward evening one day in late spring as Rosamund came across the high meadow. It was warm enough to make her wipe sweat from her forehead as she pushed through the high grass. Insects hummed away from her as she moved. The last of the men who had been out practicing were walking down the hill, and Haakon was leaning against a tree at the edge of the woods beyond the meadow. Several of the men shouted cheerful greetings when they saw Rosamund and then teased Haakon good-naturedly. Haakon shook a fist in mock anger and Rosamund smiled. There was hardly any talk now of her being a witch; some men had been heard to say that she was a good-luck sign, proving that Haakon had power from the gods to win over his enemies.

Haakon and Rosamund sat between the spreading roots of an oak and talked of the household. "I wonder if Bosa shouldn't be set free," she said. "He's done good service for twenty years, and he has a wife and son."

"Setting him free would also take away our eyes and ears in my mother's house," said Haakon.

"You still don't trust your mother?"

"I trust her. But I don't trust all of her people. Bosa can go among them where she can't and hear things she never would. I'd rather not see him leave until we've settled with Erik and Ivar."

"I'm beginning to think they've given up any idea of striking at us. I've tried to help in that. I've been making your men sound like a horde of berserkers in all my messages to Ivar."

"Good. He probably won't take just your word, though. Ivar wouldn't trust his right hand not to cut off his left."

Haakon leaned back against the tree. "If Bosa stays with my mother, he remains under my protection. If he were a free man, he'd be easier prey for Erik and Ivar. He's certainly done them enough harm to make them want his life. So he might not live to enjoy his freedom long, even if we win in the end."

"And if by some chance we lose—?"

Haakon grunted. "Don't look on the gloomy side of things."

"I can't help it. I'll be the one left alone if anything happens to you."

"True enough." Haakon clasped his hands over his knees. "If we lose, Bosa and the other thralls will be in even more danger. Some may find places with friends, but then if we lose, we won't have many friends. I doubt if anyone will put himself in danger for Bosa's sake."

"You could free him now and find him a steading somewhere beyond the Trondelag. Or is he too old to make such a new start?"

"He's as tough as this oak tree and he'll live as long. But it would break his heart to go so far. He's been only a thrall here, but the Trondelag is his home now." Haakon stood up. "I'll free Bosa and find him a steading after we've settled matters with our friends upfjord. I think he needs us now, and we surely need him."

He pulled Rosamund to her feet and helped her brush dirt and leaves from her skirt. "I want to speak with you about an important matter. We are discussing Bosa's future and whether he should be free. We have yet to discuss your future."

Rosamund shaded her eyes from the bright evening sun to see Haakon's face.

"Rosamund, I brought you here without your consent. I know very little about the family you left behind, and I want you to tell me now if you miss your homeland enough to return to it. I have no desire to keep you here against your will, and your brother will be here any time now. Do you wish to leave?"

Rosamund sighed with the remembrance of English

woods and meadows, the fragrance of clover on Ram's Head, and the sound of the sea outside her father's hold. She took Haakon's arm and turned him around so she was out of the line of the setting sun.

"Haakon, England is in my past. Soon after we met, I knew my life would be in your hands. I came with you willingly. My desire is to remain with you, if you will keep me."

"Then I will protect you against Ivar and Mark. They will have to kill me before they take you away."

Rosamund smiled at that assurance. For her part, she would gladly leave with Mark if that would save Haakon's life. *I never thought I would be blessed enough to feel this way about anyone or have anyone feel this way about me.*

Haakon threaded his fingers through his beard. He looked uncomfortable about having spoken of his love. "And now enough of this. I'm going down to the stream and get some of this dust and sweat off me. Coming?"

Hand in hand they walked into the woods to a little stream that flowed north through the trees, then along the bank to where it formed a deep pool. The water was clear and looked cold. Haakon sat down on the stump and began stripping off his clothes. "Can you swim?"

"Yes, but the men—"

"Won't be coming back. Don't worry about them seeing you." Rosamund still hesitated. She'd never been naked outdoors, unless as a child too young to remember it. Still, she'd sometimes wondered what it would feel like to have all of her skin bare to the sun and the wind. Of course there wasn't much wind here among the trees—

Too late, she saw Haakon striding toward her. He caught her around the waist and she felt his beard on her cheek.

Then he swept her into the air and dropped her into the
pool. She screamed more in surprise than in fear as she
struck the water, then thrashed so furiously that she
popped to the surface without touching bottom. "You—
you—you—" she sputtered.

"Norseman?" Haakon suggested, laughing. Before she
could reply he dove off the bank and then rose beside her
like a seal. "You'll have to get that gown off now, unless
you want to flounder like a dying whale. I'll help you."

Rosamund gripped a root on the bank and pulled herself
half out of the water. Then Haakon placed both hands on
her bottom and pushed her the rest of the way.

She sprawled face down, not sure if she should curse or
laugh. In the end she laughed. She stood up and with
fingers so steady they surprised her, she stripped off her
clothes.

She heard a sigh behind her as she finished. "Gods—I
keep forgetting how beautiful you are." She turned to see
Haakon climbing out of the pool.

"Haakon—" There had to be something more to say if
she could only think of it. But he was holding her, and
there was a tightness in her nipples and a warmth in her
belly. Then she couldn't see any real need to think of
anything as complicated as words.

With one hand he lifted her and laid her down, while
his other hand ran from her throat down across her
breasts. She wriggled to get a twig out of the small of her
back, then stopped his hands as they moved lower. As he
entered, she lifted her thighs and gripped his shoulders.
She knew that what she'd been seeking in their loving was
closer than it had ever been before. She still didn't know
how to bring it, other than by clinging as close to Haakon

as she could. The closer she held him, the more help he would give her.

So she clung as if they were a single body with two minds. She smelled Haakon's sweat, heard his heavy breathing, knew that the sun was setting on the horizon. She didn't know anything else. Before long she stopped caring.

Then thunder roared in her ears, and deep in her body bowstrings seemed to be snapping. She felt as if every one of her senses was a cup filled to overflowing. She knew that Haakon was crying out in a terrible voice and that he gripped her as tightly as she gripped him. She fainted while he still held her, although she never knew for how long.

When the world returned, she was lying on her side with her head pillowed on Haakon's chest. She moved until she could look into his eyes. They were half-closed, and from his regular breathing he seemed to be nearly asleep. She ran a hand lightly across his chest, curling some of the hair around her fingers, feeling the solid muscles and the ridges of scars.

So I've found it. She was certain of that. They'd gone on to something altogether new for them. *We have started something new. Today we have created a child; I know it as surely as we are lying here.* She sat up, shivering although the quiet air in the woods was still warm. Then she stood up and arranged her gown across a nearby bush to dry. The sound of her feet in the dry needles woke Haakon.

"Gods—what am I doing sleeping here?"

"That's a good question. What *are* you doing?"

He smacked her on the bottom, then grabbed her by

the ankle and tugged just hard enough for her to get the hint. She turned, lay down, and curled herself alongside him. After a moment he sighed.

"Who cares what we're doing here? We'll be coming here again." He stood. "Time for another swim, though."

Spray hit Rosamund as Haakon plunged into the water, and drops trickled down between her breasts. She stepped to the bank and dove in after Haakon.

XVI

Spring turned into summer without bringing any signs of activity from Mark, Ivar, or Erik. Bjorn no longer bothered to post men to guard the approaches to the steading. To be sure, Erik didn't start visiting Sigrid again, which could have been either significant or meaningless. Bosa also heard a report that one of Ivar's household had died. Last year there'd been a rumor that the same man had been asked by Erik to keep an eye on the hotheaded nephew.

"If Ivar wishes to raise hands against us, he would surely have had this man killed," said Bosa. "His death puts out Erik's eyes in his nephew's house."

Haakon shrugged. "You may be right, but two rumors don't make one truth." This didn't mean he found the waiting any easier to endure than Bosa did. Several times he'd been tempted to strike first, or at least find a way to provoke Ivar into some action that would give a reason to

destroy him. That temptation had to be resisted. Striking
first might put an end to Ivar, but it would be only the
beginning of endless quarrels with his other neighbors.
Trapping Ivar into striking first was not much better. It
would depend too much on keeping secrets. As matters
stood, Haakon had the reputation of a lawful man and Ivar
the reputation of a quarrelsome one. This was worth
another forty men or another chest of silver to Haakon—
too much to give up for uncertain gains.

Meanwhile, Haakon was busy enough. Most of the men
were as well trained as they ever would be, but there
were always the laggards. It was also good to make sure
that the rest didn't forget what they had learned. Haakon
remembered how his victory at the Ram's Head came
more from skill and stealth than from brute strength. For
this sort of work he needed men who were quick and
clearheaded, as well as strong and fearless.

Haakon also learned that Ragnar the Noseless was still
an honest man. He sent Haakon three good men, carrying
the rune-carved stick, a leather bag of silver from Hedeby,
and an invitation to join him in a trading venture in the
Baltic. They also brought Haakon a gift—a wolfhound
bitch about a year old, along with instructions to save
Ragnar one of the litter Wulf would sire.

Haakon feasted the men, counted the silver, and considered the invitation for some time before refusing. Trading in the Baltic could keep him away from home too long.
If Ivar and Mark didn't act soon, Haakon and his men
would set out for Olaf Haraldsson's steading in Ireland, as
he had pledged to his mother.

He did see about acquiring another ship to accommo-
date his new warriors. With Earl Edmund's gold and

silver, he was a wealthy man. But with ninety men eating his meat, he would not stay that way forever.

He soon found a *knarr* for sale, only a few hours' sailing from Ivar's steading. The owner was getting too stiff in the joints to sail her, while his three sons were still too young to take her to sea without him. They had nothing else in the world but their ship, so they prepared a celebration feast after Haakon offered them a generous price. He left Snorri Longfoot and half a dozen good sailors to make the *knarr* ready for sea, then returned home. He'd promised Rosamund a whole day in the woods, and he was looking forward to it himself.

Rosamund took hold of the root with one hand and covered her eyes with the other as Haakon surfaced beside her. There were times when he was as playful as a seal and threw up more water than a spouting whale. Then she let go of the root and pushed her hair out of her eyes as he caught her around the waist.

"Not in the water, for God's sake!"

"No," he said. "You'd keep slipping away. Rather like wrestling an eel, I imagine."

"But—?"

"Of course." He released Rosamund, then moved behind her to help her climb onto the bank. She fastened both hands and one foot onto the root, then he pushed hard and she bounced up onto the bank. As usual she landed flat on her face, her nose digging a hole in the soft ground. One of these days she'd have to learn to get out of the water herself, but that day wasn't here yet. She was just getting to her feet when seven men ran out of the trees at her.

She saw patched leather tunics, faded woolen trousers,

boots on two and shapeless shoes on the others, tangled hair and beards, and a weapon in each man's hand. They looked like outlaws, but Rosamund refused to believe this. *Oh, Jesus, Lord—their men are here to kill us. Haakon's still in the water, and even if he weren't, they're between him and his weapons.*

Then she screamed and ran straight at the men.

Facing the completely unexpected can make all but the best fighters hesitate, and men willing to do treacherous murder for silver aren't often the best. Seeing a beautiful naked woman charging them like a wild boar was enough to stop all seven as if they'd taken root.

By the time Rosamund reached the men, one of them was able to thrust at her with a long knife. She sidestepped the point, gripped his arm with both hands, then jerked. He didn't lose his weapon or his balance, but then she sank her teeth into his wrist as if it were a particularly juicy piece of pork. He howled and dropped the knife.

Another man gripped Rosamund around the waist from behind. She let go of the first man so suddenly that both she and her new attacker fell backward. She landed on top of him, jabbing backward with elbows and feet. One blow caught him in the throat and he gasped. Then something solid struck her in the stomach so hard all the breath went out of her. As she fought to scream, two more blows in rapid succession crashed down on her head. The world swam around her, she heard words that sounded like, "Take her and run," then there was no more world.

Rosamund's charge gave Haakon time to get out of the water and nearly reach his weapons. Then four of the men came at him. The other three grabbed Rosamund roughly

by the arms and legs and hauled her away into the woods,
dangling like the carcass of an animal.

The smallest of the four men was the boldest. He
charged at Haakon with a long knife, staying between
Haakon and the golden ax. Haakon swung his open hand
into the man's face and the knife thrust went wild. Haakon
gripped the man by the belt, picked him up, and hurled
him against his three comrades. One went down, two
leaped back, the small man lay where he fell, and Haakon's
hands closed on the handle of the golden ax.

A berserker's rage beat in his mind. The ax pumped
enormous strength into Haakon's massive arms. He raised
the ax to catch a slashing sword on the handle, then kicked
the swordsman in the groin and stepped back. His hands
flew upward, and the axhead came up into striking position, flaming gold. It sank deep into the skull of a man
with a spear that was long enough to reach Haakon first,
but didn't.

Haakon's luck nearly turned then as the ax stuck in the
man's skull and his fall jerked it out of Haakon's hands. For
a moment Haakon stood weaponless again, but the sight of
the ax buried in the spearman's skull froze the last enemy
on his feet. That gave Haakon time to snatch up a fallen
sword. With great agility he shifted to one side as the
fourth man came at him, so that the man's ax whistled
harmlessly clear. Then Haakon's borrowed sword swung in
a flat arc, cutting halfway through his attacker's left leg.
The man screamed as Haakon jumped up, screamed again
as Haakon laid open his shoulder, then collapsed silently
as Haakon's third slash chopped his head nearly off his
shoulders.

Haakon jerked his ax free and turned to the man he'd

kicked in the groin. The man had risen as far as sitting up; the ax came down on his shoulder, cutting halfway into his chest. Another jerk, the ax was free again, and Haakon turned to the small man, who was groaning and beginning to writhe. In Haakon's mind the berserker's rage was beginning to crumble.

It held long enough for Haakon to remember that he'd better ask the small man who'd sent him. He couldn't imagine anyone except Erik or Ivar doing it, but it would be better to know for certain before he called his men out. It might even be wise to leave this man alive, in case Haakon needed him to speak before the Thing.

Haakon picked up the small man's knife and bent over him, the point of the knife resting lightly on the man's groin. "If you tell me who sent you, you get a good death. Maybe you even live. If not, you die slowly, starting here." He jabbed the knife through the man's stained breeches.

The man's eyes showed only the whites, and for a moment Haakon thought he was too frightened to speak. Then he coughed, turned his head to one side, and vomited. Haakon let him spew himself empty, cursing every wasted moment. When the man could talk, Haakon repeated his question.

"Edmundsson," the man gasped. "Edmundsson and Egbertsson sent us. They paid us themselves. Didn't tell Erik. Didn't—" Haakon's fist crashed into his jaw, snapping his head back. He went limp, still breathing but as motionless as if he'd been bound hand and foot. Haakon sprang up, gripped the ax, and started to run.

He didn't run far. The trail left by the men carrying Rosamund was easy to follow, but it came to an end after only a few hundred paces. Haakon found a small clearing, the grass trampled down and matted with horse drop-

pings, and nothing else. Rosamund's captors had turned
loose the horses of their dead comrades. Haakon couldn't
expect to catch one, and chasing mounted men on foot was
hopeless.

He called himself filthy names. The horses must have
been tethered here while he and Rosamund were in the
pool. This was close enough so that if he'd been properly
on guard, he should have heard something. His mind and
his ears had been elsewhere, and now Rosamund was in
Mark's and Ivar's hands.

The thought broke hard against his rage. There were no
human enemies or even their horses to feel it, so the ax
sank into the trees around the clearing. Metal rang,
splinters the size of a man's hand flew, small trees fell at a
single blow, branches and leaves rained down. Haakon's
rage was exhausted only when a tree as thick as his own
body came down nearly on top of him.

He stood for a moment, rivers of sweat pouring off his
naked body, hair and beard tangled, his mouth still working and his eyes terrifying in their rage. Then he swung
the golden ax up onto his shoulder and began to retrace
his steps. As he did, his thoughts began to flow again. At
least it didn't seem that Erik was implicated. That equal-
ized the odds and would also make Sigrid happy. The first
thing to do was to pretend that he'd been seriously
wounded. That would put Mark and Ivar off their guard,
and help gain the surprise he would need. . . .

Rosamund regained consciousness sooner than she, in
retrospect, would have expected. She opened her eyes
slowly, fearful of what she might see. A man stood before
her, his identity concealed by the darkness of the chamber.

"Rosamund! Are you all right?"

Oh, Mother Mary. Mark. "Yes, yes, I am all right, no thanks to your imbeciles. What are you trying to prove by this madness? How brave you are? What a fine warrior?" Rosamund tried to sit up, but the pain in the back of her head prevented it. In disgust she sank slowly down into the pillows.

"Aren't you even going to thank me? Aren't you glad I've come to rescue you?"

"Oh, Mark, did you do this for me or for your reputation? What makes you so sure I want to be rescued...except maybe from you."

"What are you saying? You are out of your senses from the blow to your head. In the morning, you will feel much better when we sail for England."

"Idiot! I am sailing nowhere."

"You would stay here with a godless man in this wretched country? Besides, you have no choice. You are betrothed to Harud Olafsson who has agreed in good faith not to release you and Father from the marriage agreement. You will be delivered to him when we return to England, in exchange for the price already paid to Ivar Egbertsson. And when Ivar wins Haakon's lands, he will share the wealth with Harud. It's funny really, when you think of it: Olaf Haraldsson devastates Haakon's father, and his son follows suit in the next generation."

Mark began to dissolve into a mindless, high-pitched laughter that was too much for Rosamund to bear.

"No! You would have to kill me first before I would go to Harud. Haakon will come for me. He will not let you take me away...not when I am carrying his child—"

Mark slapped her hard across the mouth, pulled her from the bed, and slammed her against the wall.

"You whore! You dog! What filth have you turned into?"

The pain roared in Rosamund's head and white flashes burst before her eyes just before she lost consciousness.

Rosamund awoke and found herself tied hand and foot, lying facedown across the back of a horse. The horse was moving at a trot and shaking her so badly that for a while she couldn't be sure if she was hurt or not. She finally decided that she wasn't, although she was still naked and every so often branches lashed her back or legs.

She tried to twist her head around and get a good look at her captors, but discovered that she was bound too tightly. At least the tight bindings kept her from falling under the fast-moving hooves. Certainly she couldn't hope to outrun these men even if she did somehow get free. She was a captive again, and in far more danger than she'd faced at the Ram's Head.

She knew she could reduce that danger, however. She would swallow her pride and her rage and be the tamest captive Ivar could hope for. That would win time—time for Mark and Ivar to fall out, time for Haakon's men to gather and strike. She was certain that armed men would be on their way to her rescue within a day or two, whether Haakon survived the attack or not.

There was another reason for staying alive at any cost: She was carrying Haakon's child. If he lived and came to free her with the golden ax in his hands, the child would bind them together in a way nothing could break. If Haakon was dead, she would live to bear the child and then raise it to be proud of the way its father had died and its mother had fought her enemies.

XVII

Ivar Egbertsson threw down his drinking horn so hard at Mark Edmundsson's feet that it cracked. He would have liked to have thrown it at Mark's head, but he wasn't quite drunk or angry enough to forget himself completely.

"You *don't know* if Haakon's dead or not?"

"None of the four who stayed to fight him came back. But four against one—"

"May not have been enough against Haakon. Why didn't those fools who took Rosamund leave her and go back?"

"I don't know. They may have thought—"

"*Thought?*" Ivar made the word sound like an obscenity.

"Ivar, you owe me plenty—in gold and men. Don't think you are so grand. Without me, you're nothing. If Haakon's alive, he will walk into our hands."

"And he's a man to be reckoned with. So you finally understand that you've put us in danger. How wise of you. If you'd only been that wise a few days ago . . ." With a shudder, Ivar rose to his feet, and looked down at his accomplice. "Well, it's done. Your people have Rosamund?"

"Yes."

"Is she badly hurt?"

"Not as badly as I would have liked, the whore."

"That doesn't answer my question."

"She doesn't seem to be badly hurt, but we'll have to
179

postpone leaving until her bruises heal. Neither my father nor Harud will be happy with the condition she's in. Also, I want one of your healing women to do something about the Dane's bastard she's carrying before we set sail."

"Good enough. Where is she?"

"At the Ravens' Perch, just as we had planned."

Ivar cursed. The Ravens' Perch was a crag high above the Trondheimsfjord, about half a morning's brisk walk to the west of his steading. The only approach to it lay up a winding path across a steep, boulder-strewn slope. The hut on the crag once sheltered men keeping watch for pirates on the fjord.

"You've put your men there?"

"Of course, Ivar. I'm not a fool, in spite of what you think. Even if I were, a fool can learn if he sees the truth often enough. I've seen your ways often enough to know what you're thinking."

"Oh? Has Rosamund taught you spells to see into my mind?"

Mark ignored the taunt. "You want to take Rosamund to your own bed, don't you? You'd like to kill me and Haakon so she'll be your little prize."

Ivar grunted. Mark was showing too much wisdom now. If he'd only had the wisdom to go with his men and see that they did their work, Haakon might now be dead. Mark could have been dead as well, but Ivar would have shed no tears over that. As it was, Mark had given too much importance to making it seem Haakon died at the hands of outlaws. He would not go with his men, they left their work undone, and now matters were far more desperate than before.

"Very well. I will send some of my men up to join

yours. You can't have enough there. Haakon could easily snatch Rosamund and then be free to do as he chooses with both of us."

Perhaps there was a way of getting Rosamund into his own hands. Right now he was too tired, too drunk, and too angry to think of one. He'd sleep and hope that the morning brought greater wisdom instead of a shipload of Haakon's men howling for blood.

Bjorn shut the door and came over to Haakon's bed. Haakon slowly turned his head. If he moved quickly, the bandages wrapped around one leg, one arm, his chest, and his head all tightened painfully. He could hardly have been less able to move if he really had been wounded in several places.

"We can talk now, Haakon," said Bjorn.

"Good." Haakon looked around the room, which also held Knut the One-Eye, Gunnar, and his mother. He winced as the poultice under the bandages on his chest dried, tangled, and pulled hairs out by the roots. For the tenth time he wished he'd been able to think of a better trick to put Ivar off his guard. However, time had been short, and Haakon knew that a good plan made in time is better than the best made a day late.

"My first order is for Bjorn," Haakon began. "Bring in all the guards you've sent out."

"Haakon, if they come in, Ivar and Mark may surprise us. They could certainly put their men close enough around this steading to prevent us from surprising them."

"I don't believe those two will be able to agree on strategy for at least a day or two. Meanwhile, I don't want our men tired from watching all night."

Bjorn looked ready to argue, so Haakon spoke sharply. "Bjorn, stop flogging yourself. You didn't put the guards out before because I didn't tell you to. What happened is as much my fault as yours. Bring our men in. Besides, I have a plan that should give us the advantage of surprise even if Ivar has men watching us."

Bjorn looked willing to listen, and Haakon continued. "By dawn of the day after tomorrow, Rosamund or at least someone who knows where she is will surely be at Ivar's steading. So far, we know no one has sailed from there. And we also know that Ivar has not contacted his uncle for help. I think we have a good chance to raid Ivar's steading at dawn, going by the fjord."

"If Ivar sends spies, he'll see that the ships are gone," said Bjorn. He still wasn't completely giving up his fight.

"You forget the *knarr* upfjord," said Haakon. "Snorri and his men should have her ready, and Ivar doesn't know that she's now ours. This far from the sea, she can carry fifty men. We'll leave here aboard *Red Hawk* after darkness falls. She's fast enough to take us to the *knarr* by midnight. I will go with the men on a litter. Then we can put our people aboard the *knarr* while *Red Hawk* sails home and I throw off my disguise. By dawn *Red Hawk* will be back where she was at sunset. Meanwhile, an innocent *knarr* will be sailing up to Ivar's steading.

"We'll be leaving half our men on guard here, so one of you has to lead them. Bjorn, I won't ask you. You're too determined to win back the honor you've lost by not setting out the guards. Gunnar—"

"Haakon, let me come with you," said the poet. "Guthrun has spoken plainly. If I am not among the first into the battle to save her lady, I will never wed her. What is more, she will make me unfit to wed any other woman as well."

"Very well, Gunnar. Your manhood is safe. You'll be with me. Knut? . . ."

The one-eyed man looked resigned to his fate. "The work you have given me must be done, even though it is safe. If no one thinks I am holding back from this honorable fight—"

Sigrid laughed. "Knut, you couldn't hold back from a fight as long as you could move your limbs. Your soul was cut to the same measure as my son's, for better or worse."

"And—when we reach Ivar's steading?" said Gunnar.

"We find Rosamund," said Haakon, in a voice like boulders grinding together in the surf. "We find Rosamund and bring her home." He would not tempt bad luck by adding, "Alive or dead." The others would understand what he'd left unsaid, and also what would happen to Mark and Ivar and their men if Rosamund did not come home alive.

Rosamund curled herself as tightly as the chain on her leg would let her and listened to the wind piping outside the hut. It was a thin and lonely sound, and she preferred the voices of the men around the campfire, even if they were enemies. They were at least living men, not ghosts, and she'd learned a good deal from listening to them.

She'd learned that Haakon was not dead, but so badly wounded that he might yet die. Certainly he would not be fighting again this year. That would not keep his men from coming after her, but would they have the same chance of success without Haakon leading them?

A burning log cracked and she heard shuffling feet.

Most of the men guarding her were Ivar Egbertsson's. She didn't know if this was good or bad. Certainly Mark wanted her alive to return to Harud. If the men were Mark's, they certainly would not let her escape. But Ivar wouldn't care particularly if she were alive or dead. That could work against her. If she caused any trouble, Ivar might have her killed and then say she'd sailed with her brother.

Rosamund shifted to ease her cramped and bruised limbs. She felt straw prick her cheek and the gown tug painfully at the blood clots over the wounds she'd received from lashing branches during the ride through the forest. At least her captors seemed ready to keep her alive for now. The hut was freshly cleaned, she had a tattered wool gown to wear and straw to lie on, and they'd fed her porridge and a bit of pork. She was filthy, cold, and hurting all over, but she knew she could live for weeks like this if she had to.

Rosamund's thoughts were interrupted by the hut door opening. A guard walked in, leading an old woman with tangled, gray hair. *She looks a century old. Is she also a prisoner?* Rosamund watched as the woman set down a sack of hide, closed with a leather thong.

"This is the lady," the guard said. The old woman peered at Rosamund through the dark, then nodded.

"Boiling water," the woman instructed in a hoarse whisper. The guard nodded, then left.

The gnarled, leathery hands untied the knot and spread various leaves, seeds, and twigs onto the ground.

"Are you a healer?" Rosamund asked. *Perhaps Mark is feeling some remorse for the beating. As well he should.*

The woman turned her head slightly, permitting Rosamund

the full view of her face. After a barely perceptible nod, the old woman returned to her work.

"You must have come for my wounds. Thank you. I admit, I am feeling rather sore," Rosamund confided. *Perhaps if I make friends, she will help me.*

The guard returned carrying a small iron pot filled almost to overflowing with steaming water. The woman motioned for him to set it down next to her. He positioned it carefully, then stood back to observe. The woman looked up, outraged by his continued presence. After one look at her expression, he fled the hut.

Using her skirt to protect her hands from the pot's heat, the woman spilled half the water onto the ground. She chose several herbs, held them between her palms, then rubbed her palms together so the crushed leaves floated down into the pot. Rosamund watched with interest. Next, the woman added one powder and then another. The small hut was filled with a noxious, bitter odor that made Rosamund gag. This soup was stirred with a twig, which was then dropped into the pot. The woman turned her head slightly toward Rosamund.

"You will drink half of this liquor, then we will wait for you to vomit," she whispered. "After you vomit, we will pour the rest of the liquor into you. In twice the time it takes you to vomit, you will lose the child."

Rosamund looked at the woman, in shock.

"No! I will not! You cannot make me!"

A slight smile curled at the lips of the old woman as she moved toward Rosamund. "You will not?" she whispered. "But I believe you will."

"Watch the spear point!"

"Stop pushing, curse you. I'm almost over the side."

"Quiet, or they'll hear you on the other side of the fjord!"

From where he sat propped against a stump, Haakon could easily follow the loading of the *knarr* by the noise. It was going well enough, considering that they didn't dare show a light and that nearly fifty armed men were being packed like herring into a ship that would have been crowded with thirty. So far only one man had fallen into the water.

Wulf came over and licked Haakon's face. Haakon raised his free arm and scratched the wolfhound's head. He would rather have left the dog behind, but Wulf's familiarity with Rosamund's scent might be needed to locate her. The dog had leaped aboard *Red Hawk* at the last moment, whined piteously at Haakon, and growled ominously at everyone else. Haakon didn't have the heart to put him ashore, and no one else dared to try.

At last the noise from the ship died. Haakon threw off the fur covering him and stood up. Wulf stared at his master, then started barking wildly, rose on his hind legs, and put both paws on Haakon's shoulder. Haakon nearly went over backward. Bjorn gripped Wulf's collar, and Wulf would have taken Bjorn's hand off at the wrist if he hadn't missed when he snapped at Bjorn.

Haakon stretched arms and legs to loosen muscles and joints. Then he pulled on his tunic and trousers.

"Haakon!"

Haakon wheeled around; no one was supposed to know he was here. He saw Bosa running up to him, panting from the exertion. Haakon had to wait patiently before the thrall could speak.

"Haakon, there is one who would like to join you

waiting at the bottom of the hill. Should I bring him to you?"

"Who is this man, Bosa? Can he not wait until we return? This is a strange time for a warrior to swear loyalty."

"You will understand when you know who it is. It is—"

"It is Erik the Bald." Haakon looked past Bosa to see the speaker striding up the hill.

Haakon darted a look at Bosa, who shrugged sheepishly.

"Haakon Olesson, it is my intention to join you. I have learned what my nephew has done, and I swear to you that I knew nothing about it. I have misjudged Ivar. That much is clear. My coming with you tonight will help me redeem myself in your eyes, and in the eyes of your mother."

Haakon did not believe he would be doing his men a favor by bringing Erik along. Although he had no proof of the man's guilt, neither did he have proof of his innocence.

"I will also swear an oath that if your mother will marry me after this shame of my nephew's, and if she should die before me, all of her land will go to you. My nephew is no longer my kin. I will have nothing more to do with him."

Haakon did not know what to do. It was possible that Erik's worst crime was loyalty to his family. Now that he was willing to forswear the lands— Yet, this could be a plot. Erik might have been sent by Ivar to undermine the scheme for Rosamund's rescue. . . .

Abruptly, Haakon's ears were filled with the rushing wind, and he could no longer hear his own thoughts. The roar whirled about his head and Haakon feared he might lose his footing and tumble heels over head down the length of the hill. He reached out to steady himself.

"Haakon! What is wrong?" Bosa took hold of Haakon's shoulders.

"It is the wind. I couldn't hear for the wind," Haakon said, then realized there was no wind. Bosa and Erik exchanged glances. "Erik, you will join us tonight. A man's character should be judged by his own behavior, not by that of another. I will accept your oath that my mother's lands, should you and she marry, will come to me if she dies before you."

It needed twenty men pushing with all their strength at her bow before the overloaded *knarr* was afloat. Haakon and Erik were the last of the twenty to climb aboard. They went forward to pull on their armor as the oars splashed into the water on either side. From amidships came thuds and scraping noises as men readied the sail for hoisting as soon as the oarsmen took them clear of the land. Haakon wrung the water out of his beard and for the first time in days felt like smiling.

XVIII

Rosamund awoke cold, hungry, thirsty, and stiff and aching in every limb. The potion had caused her to wretch beyond the point of dry heaves, but she did not know for certain the liquor's effect on her unborn child. She longed for a hot bath or even some warm butter to spread on her battered hide. Then she heard Mark's voice outside the hut. *He is truly his father's son;* Rosamund laughed bitterly.

It would have never occurred to him to protect her. The old woman was likely his idea.

Mark seemed to be questioning the guards about her and was getting surly replies from Ivar's men. Her two captors were probably no better friends than ever. She could hardly hope to gain any advantage from their quarrel, however—at least not while they held her at the Ravens' Perch. She was locked up, chained, shoeless, scantily clothed, and surrounded by armed men who certainly thought they were being unusually kind by not passing her around among themselves.

For a moment the thought of the odds against her was almost unbearably grim. Still, she did not weep. She *would* not; her anger was too great to give in to despair. She desperately wished she could go back to sleep in order to forget, but she knew the guards would be coming in soon to give her the morning meal. Her sense of dignity insisted she be awake to face them.

Ignoring the talk of the men outside, she slowly grew calm again. It seemed to be a cloudy day with little wind and no fog. From the Ravens' Perch a man could see all the way to Ivar's steading and well out into the fjord beyond. She heard one man point out a *knarr* creeping along just offshore, and another saying that it seemed to be putting in at Ivar's steading.

Haakon lay on his back on the *knarr*'s deck and looked up at Snorri Longfoot, who was standing in the bow and playing ship's captain. He seemed to be thoroughly enjoying himself, even though he'd had to shave off his beard and trim his hair to make sure he wouldn't be recognized.

"A hundred paces more, Haakon."

Only Haakon heard Snorri's whisper, but everyone on deck, standing or lying down out of sight, heard the hail from the shore. "*Hoaaa*, the *knarr*. This is the steading of Ivar Egbertsson! What do you want?"

"We struck a rock before dawn and started a plank," Snorri shouted. "The water's knee-deep in the hold already. Let us land and lighten ship, and maybe borrow some tools and timber."

"You'll find Ivar's hospitality thin," was the response from the shore. "We're at feud with Haakon Olesson downfjord."

Snorri shrugged. "I haven't heard about that." Without looking down at Haakon, Snorri held out five fingers by his side to indicate the number of men waiting on shore.

"What weapons?" Haakon whispered.

"Three spears, an ax, a sword."

"Ready the archers."

Snorri raised his arms over his head, crossed them, then shouted, "You fools! Do you want us to sink here in front of your eyes because your chief's afraid of strangers? Let us land and you can look us over. If you help us save the cargo, you'll find yourselves richer for it." Ivar's greed was common knowledge. Snorri's offer should silence any man in Ivar's service.

Then Snorri whispered again, "Fifty paces, Haakon."

Haakon hurled himself to his feet and six of his best archers rose with him, bows strung and quivers full. Snorri and the rowers threw themselves flat on the deck as the archers nocked arrows and shot. Haakon remained standing, arrows whistling past his ears. Three of the men went down like stones, one collapsed with a scream, the last turned and bolted toward Ivar's steading as if monsters

were pursuing him from out of the fjord. The archers
nocked again, but the *knarr* ran aground as they shot. The
men staggered forward, out of balance, and all of their
arrows missed.

"Don't waste any more arrows," Haakon shouted. "Let's
get ashore!" He gripped the golden ax in both hands and
sprang over the side. The ax came to life as Haakon flexed
his fingers around the handle. The archers followed him,
holding their weapons over their heads to keep the bowstrings dry. With clatters and splashes the rest of Haakon's
men followed. A few of the shorter ones went completely
under, but struggled safely into shallower water to be
pulled out by their comrades. The thirty men who'd spent
the hours since daylight packed in the hold would have
fought wolves barehanded for a breath of fresh air. They
clambered ashore to find the nearest enemy five hundred
paces away.

Haakon bent over the only one of Ivar's men still able to
speak. "You can save yourself by answering one question.
Where is the lady Rosamund Edmundsdottír?"

The man gasped for air. "I—ahhhh—she's at the Ravens'
Perch. Edmundsson's and Ivar's men—ah!" Blood trickled
as he bit his lip from the pain; then he tried to summon
the strength to point. Instead, he indicated the direction
by rolling his pain-filled eyes. Haakon nodded and sig-
naled his men to carry the prisoners aboard the *knarr*. He
knew where the Ravens' Perch was. Ivar had made an
excellent choice for his purpose; huge boulders would
afford his troops much protection and a narrow pass would
be easy to defend. If they started off at once, they could
reach it before Ivar could either catch up with them or
send reinforcements to the Perch. Of course they would

be cut off from the shore, but that was no great danger.
Haakon's steading was only two days' march, and there
were any number of good places along the way to stand
and fight if necessary.

By now the *knarr* was afloat again, being rowed along
the shore to where Ivar's longship *Dragon Queen* lay. As
Gunnar and Bjorn counted the men, Haakon watched two
of Snorri's strongest warriors, armed with axes, jump
overboard from the *knarr* and wade to the longship. They
chopped enough holes in *Dragon Queen* to keep her out of
the day's fracas.

Haakon again surveyed Ivar's steading. The man who
fled from the shore should be arriving soon, bringing
warning. More smoke seemed to be rising, but that was
all. Was Ivar refusing battle for now, and if so, why?
Haakon wondered if Egbertsson expected him to rescue
Rosamund, slaughter Mark's men, then fall into a trap as
he came down from the Perch. It wouldn't be beyond
Ivar's treachery to leave Mark and his men in the lurch.
Well, if the path to Rosamund lay clear, he would gladly
take his chances with the trap afterward.

Bits of gravel bit into Rosamund's legs and one hip, and
she knew that the cuts on her back were open and
bleeding again. One cheek was also raw and burning. But
it was still worth the pain in order to see what was going
on around her. The blindfold no longer covered her eyes,
but none of the men seemed to have noticed.

They had bound her hands behind her back and put the
blindfold on her before they had loosed the chain and led
her out of the hut. She had gulped the fresh air, and even
with the blindfold, the slight glare slipping under the cloth

had seared her eyes. She stumbled and fell several times as they led her hurriedly over the rocky slopes. After she fell the third time, they bound her feet as well and carried her the rest of the way. She knew this was not from any kindness, but because they were pressed for time.

She knew this from hearing the curses of the men as they moved faster, and she thought she knew why. Haakon's men must have landed, and hopefully, some of them were on their way up to the Ravens' Perch. Ivar's men had abandoned it, but she didn't know where they had taken her. Certainly they hadn't sounded like men retreating. She'd heard the scrape of weapons being sharpened and the men digging in rather than running away. At last she knew she had to see, even if she died for it. So she lay down and went to work to shift the blindfold.

What she saw at last was Mark and a dozen armed men crouching behind boulders. Beyond the boulders, the hillside dropped steeply, and far away she could see a sweeping, majestic view of the fjord. Some of the boulders looked as if a good shove would send them careening down the hill onto anyone coming up from below. Four of the men were archers with bows strung and arrows laid out ready to hand.

This told her enough. There were places on the path up to the Ravens' Perch where a dozen men could easily make a stand against fifty. Mark and his men had found one of those places and were waiting there for Ivar and his men to join them, and for Haakon's men to come at them. To be sure, Mark would learn that no hillside full of rocks would keep away Haakon's men, but the fight might be long and bloody. Rosamund wished they hadn't bound her ankles. Otherwise she would have considered running

when the fight began, instead of lying there nearly help-
less. Mark was doomed and might find a chance to kill
her—to preserve the family honor—before he himself
went down.

Rosamund saw Mark move quickly among his men,
making certain of strategies and also assuring them that
Ivar would soon join their ranks with his own forces.

"Do not be a fool, Mark. I know all about Ivar Egbertsson.
He will save himself today with not a thought about you.
Go home Mark, you and your men, before it is too late."

Mark Edmundsson looked down at his sister, his eyes
hot coals. "Women do not understand honor. You have
tumbled with this Norseman, like a slave girl, even though
you were already betrothed. Do not tell me what to do."

"I am your blood kin. Please listen to me. I—"

"I will hear no more from a whore. You will be gagged if
I hear another word."

There was no appealing to her brother's sympathy,
Rosamund realized, nor certainly to his common sense.
She would have to depend upon herself and Haakon—or,
if he was dead, on his men—to save her. Whatever
happened to Mark now was his own fate and she absolved
herself of any responsibility.

She was testing the binding on her ankles when she
heard a dog barking from somewhere down the hill. Her
breath nearly stopped. It was Wulf's bark. Haakon was
here, alive, and at the head of his men. She knew Wulf
would never follow anyone except her or Haakon. Then
she saw the archers readying their arrows and Rosamund
knew what she had to do. Mark's men would surely make
Haakon their first target, and the odds would be against
even the best fighter if he was caught by surprise.

Rosamund twisted and struggled until she could sit up. The scraping of gravel made Mark turn around. Before he could do more, Rosamund sucked in all the air she could, then let it out in a desperate scream: "*Haakon!*"

As he trotted up the hill, Haakon was looking more forward than backward. He hadn't completely forgotten Ivar's men, but it was difficult to think of them as posing a threat. He'd only seen a dozen of them since his men moved inland, and only six closed within bowshot. Hagar the Simple killed three of them with four arrows and the others heeded the warning and fell back. That made seven of Ivar's men dead or prisoners with not a scratch on any of Haakon's. They were decreasing the odds they'd face if it came to a battle. Haakon still rather hoped it would not—he did not want Rosamund to be endangered—but he would not turn aside of the battle game after Rosamund was safe.

The path turned. Far ahead Haakon saw a hut and a smouldering campfire. There was no sign of Mark's men, which was all that kept Haakon from running to the small shelter. He took two long strides and was in the middle of a third when he heard Rosamund's scream.

So did Wulf. His mouth opened more like a shark's than a dog's. His eyes seemed to glow like the golden ax, his hair bristled until he looked twice his normal size. Then he launched himself up the hill faster than Haakon had ever seen a dog move. Haakon was so amazed by Wulf's speed that he wasn't among the first of his men to follow the dog. That honor went to Gunnar, and several more men, including Erik, were also charging the boulders before Haakon swung the golden ax off his shoulder and followed them.

Mark emerged from between two boulders, signaling to his archers. They assailed Haakon's warriors with arrows. One of Haakon's men was hit in the neck, another tore an arrow out of his leather coat and charged ahead. Mark put his shoulder to a boulder, hoping to send it crashing toward the Norse, but saw Wulf coming at him, and instead drew his sword. A moment later he realized Wulf was too close. Mark dropped the sword, drew his knife, and crouched, poised to meet Wulf's spring. Wulf soared into the air and the knife flashed up to meet him. Wulf snarled viciously as he came down, Mark screamed, then frothing jaws that could tear the throat out of a stag closed on the man's neck. Mark was thrashing futilely under Wulf as the dog pulled him upward and rattled the man back and forth. Mark's back arched and his body was tossed about like a rag doll. Haakon ran past them, scanning in every direction to find Rosamund.

He found her, leaning against a boulder, with a spearman hovering over her, meeting her terrified gaze with a sadistic smirk. The spear's point moved down toward its mark. Haakon swung the golden ax at the full stretch of his arm. The ax hewed through the man's armor and spine, his spear dug into the ground beside Rosamund, and he crashed on top of her. Rosamund screamed, and Haakon pulled the body off her and held her so tightly she squealed, while his men swarmed in among the boulders.

Haakon's men gave no quarter as fierce combat ensued. The rock-hard ground became slippery with greasy blood and at times it was difficult to differentiate friend from foe. The last of Mark's men was fleeing up the path toward the hut when Erik caught him with a spear. The man wasn't mortally hurt, but the spear knocked him down and sent him rolling off the path onto the slope. The slope steepened, and he rolled faster and faster, tumbling down the incline. As he realized he wasn't going to stop, he screamed and was still screaming when he somersaulted over the edge of the cliff.

Haakon moved to Mark's motionless body. He took hold of Wulf's paw. The dog licked Haakon's hand, then whimpered softly and closed his eyes. When Haakon carefully lifted Wulf away from Mark's body, Rosamund finally began to cry. The hound was wounded, but the stab was not serious, so Haakon comforted Rosamund as well as he could, then began counting up his dead and wounded. He was finishing this grim task when Bjorn hurried up from the rear. "I'm sorry we finished this pack before you had—" Haakon began, but Bjorn stopped him with a laugh.

"Everyone's going to have his fair share of fighting before long. Look down there." Haakon's eyes followed Bjorn's finger, and he saw a dark cluster of men forming at the bottom of the hill. More were hurrying up from the shore to join them. Whether Ivar had been setting a trap or had merely been slow in bringing the rest of his men up, he was now on hand and ready for a fight.

Haakon knew he could probably still get his men away without a battle here on the hill. Rosamund, poor Wulf, and Mark's head wouldn't weigh them down much. But his men had their blood up, they'd cut down the odds against them still more, and Ivar's men would have to attack uphill.

Haakon looked down at the beach by the steading.

Dragon Queen was lying where she'd been, but another boat was putting out from shore. It looked heavily laden, and Haakon doubted it could overtake the *knarr* unless the wind died completely. At the worst, Snorri and the others could beach the *knarr* on the far shore of the fjord and hide in the woods. They would lose the ship but would probably save themselves. Meanwhile, the men in only one boat would be that many fewer Ivar could bring to the fight on the hill.

"We'll fight," he said, half to himself, then started issuing orders. His first order was to make the wounded as comfortable as possible—and he had to shout at Rosamund to keep her from getting up and helping men less hurt than she. Then Haakon spread word that they were to take full advantage of the hiatus: Everyone was to sit down, take off his helmet, divide up the water, eat if he was hungry. Everyone was to examine his weapons, and anyone who needed a new one should ask Bjorn—he'd stripped their dead enemies. Guards were to watch the enemy, with a few archers standing ready to help them.

"Then we are going downhill and make a feast for the ravens, with Ivar Egbertsson as the main dish."

As Ivar led his men within bowshot of Haakon's, his strongest desire was to be somewhere else. He had no more than fifty of his own men to face forty of Haakon's. His own men were uneasy and shifty eyed, while Haakon's looked as sure of themselves as a band of men facing a band of half-grown boys. Mark Edmundsson was nowhere to be seen, and most of the Englishmen were dead. A dozen of his own best were off chasing that cursed *knarr*. Mark had promised Harud Olafsson's aid, but Ivar had never been certain whether this was true or merely a lie to obtain a commitment against Haakon. In any case, Olafsson was probably safe in Ireland with his men, awaiting his encounter with Haakon there. Ivar had counted on this assistance that had never arrived, and now he knew there was little hope for victory. Even if Ivar won this fight, it was long odds against his having enough men left to make any use of the victory. He would fight, though, if only to keep the taunt of "coward" from following him to the end of his life.

Ivar shouted the first challenge. "Haakon Darkling! You and your men are dung on my land. They are foul and stinking above it, but soon they will be below."

"What ails you, Ivar, to make you so full of wind?" Haakon taunted back. "But you were always better with your mouth than with your sword!" Ivar bit his lip. Then Haakon raised his ax.

"Men of Ivar Egbertsson! I am here because your chief made a lawless attack on me and forcefully took away my lady. I have taken all the vengeance needed for that. No man who stands out of my path this day need fear me or my men. By Thor and by this ax I swear it."

One of Ivar's men shouted, "What about weregild for those you slew already?"

"Your chief has unlawfully taken money in exchange for stealing my woman and making her a prisoner. If he returns it, I shall divide it to pay weregild for all of Ivar's men who have died today. By Thor and by this ax I swear it."

Ivar's reply was a growl. "Haakon, a whore brought you into the world, so a whore should bury you. I'll let Rosamund do that work before I take her for myself. Now

stand forth from your men and fight *me*. Then we'll see
who feeds the ravens."

Ivar saw Rosamund turn white and stagger. Bjorn gripped
Haakon by the arms. Haakon pulled Bjorn's hands loose
and placed them on Rosamund's shoulders, speaking a few
words to Rosamund and Bjorn that Ivar couldn't hear.
Then he raised the ax and stepped closer. As Haakon came
closer, Ivar saw that his face was extraordinarily calm,
although his hair and beard were tangled and wild. His
shield was almost unmarked, and he held the largest ax
Ivar had ever seen anyone use one-handed.

Haakon was immensely relieved to find Ivar willing to
meet him in single combat. Whoever fed the ravens now,
there would be fewer widows and orphans from this day's
fighting. He was spared the danger of a victory made
barren by the amount of blood spilled in winning it.

On the other hand, he'd done nothing to improve his
own chances of seeing another sunset. In spite of the
insults he'd thrown at Ivar, Haakon knew the man was a
formidable opponent—bigger, possibly stronger, certainly
as agile, and definitely with a longer reach. Right now Ivar
was also probably fresher, and fighting for his reputation
and honor among his own men as well as for his life would
make him do his best. Haakon hoped that knowing his
own men were watching would make Ivar fight honorably,
but Haakon would not wager much on that.

So before he went forward, Haakon had spoken briefly
to Bjorn and Rosamund. "If I fall, take care of Rosamund.
Give her whatever she asks, and offer yourself as a husband. Also, repeat my offer of peace and weregild to Ivar's
men. They won't be able to stand against us if we all

choose to fight against them, and they know it. The fewer of them we kill today, the less chance we'll have of blood-feuds and the more chance of peace. With Ivar still alive and with me dead, you'd need that help."

Haakon was quite sure that if Ivar killed him today, it would do Ivar little good in the end. Bjorn, Rosamund, Gunnar, Knut, and his mother together were more than a match for Ivar, a fact the man would quickly learn. Nonetheless, Haakon wanted to win today. A nearly bloodless victory could still be barren if a warrior did not live to gather its fruits.

Haakon fit his large, strong right hand around the ax handle and flexed his fingers. The axhead glowed with pulsating light. Haakon began the fight with both ax and shield because he wanted the shield's defense while he tested Ivar's strength and speed. What he learned then would guide him in deciding whether or not to shift to using the golden ax two-handed. Rosamund's life and freedom were in no real danger now, so he had nothing to gain by fighting like a berserker. Rather than allowing his emotions to take control, he would use his mind.

Ivar's sword whipped out before Haakon thought he was within striking distance. The tip gouged splinters from Haakon's shield, and sparks flew from the bronzed iron boss in the center. His shield arm quivered, even though Ivar was striking at full stretch. Closer in, that blow might have beaten his shield aside. Haakon decided to keep his distance and watch Ivar wear himself down. But Ivar wasn't about to fall into that game. Instead, he took one step forward and his sword slashed down. Haakon's shield rose to meet it. More splinters flew, and the golden ax whizzed toward Ivar's outstretched arm. Ivar jerked his

arm and sword back, while Haakon pulled back the ax and
stepped to the right. Ivar mirrored his opponent's movements, then struck from the side. This time he missed
Haakon's shield completely, but he was also out of reach of
the golden ax. Again the two men moved to Haakon's
right, and this time Haakon struck first even though he
wasn't sure he'd hit anything. Ivar's sword glanced harmlessly
off the handle of the golden ax. A moment later both men
had their weapons drawn back and their shields raised
again.

Shifting their footing continuously and striking at nearly
full stretch, the two men made five complete circles. Half
of the time Ivar was facing uphill, the other half of the
time Haakon was at the same disadvantage. Ivar's longer
reach meant he struck Haakon's shield more often, but
Haakon's ax struck harder when it landed. Both shields
were beginning to look rat-gnawed, and both men were
shiny with sweat.

Haakon trained most of his attention on Ivar without
ignoring the men standing around watching. His own men
would probably understand why he fought at a distance,
but he wasn't sure about Ivar's. If they started calling him
coward, he would have to close in somewhat to keep Ivar
from gaining new courage. If they started abusing Ivar
about the distance he maintained, Haakon would have to
be alert for a berserker's rush. Ivar had been known to
lose his temper in a fight even when there was much less
at stake than there was today.

The circling went on. The watching men were silent,
but Haakon began to think it might not be wise to keep
his distance much longer. Ivar had started out fresher and
now showed no more signs of tiring than if he'd been made

of the same rock as the mountainside underfoot. Haakon knew that the same wasn't true of him. Before much longer he might be too slow to take advantage of a sudden opening, or to defend against an equally sudden attack. Although the golden ax sustained his physical strength, his mental exhaustion could take its toll. He shortened his grip on the golden ax and took two steps toward Ivar. Now many strokes that before would have crashed against shields came down on armor. Both struck harder blows than before. Haakon only struck when he could be sure of landing a clean blow. Dwarf work or not, the golden ax wouldn't do its work alone. It had to be directed by a fearless, strong warrior.

The fight was a brutal endurance contest. Blows came down on Haakon's helmet, making his ears ring. But the helmet partly parried the force of the blows. More hacking crashed his ribs and belly, driving the breath out of him. He fought to regain his breath; otherwise, he'd become easy prey for his adversary. He knew there'd be bruises; he hoped there'd be nothing worse. Haakon could barely see for the sweat and dirt pouring into his eyes. Their men formed a blurred circle around the leaders and were involuntarily offering encouragement or emulating the movements of the fighters in their intense involvement with the struggle.

Then one blow landed on Haakon's right shoulder. For a moment the arm was numb. He felt blood flowing where mail rings gouged flesh, and he desperately shook life back into the arm. Before he could raise it again, Ivar recognized Haakon's weakness and his opportunity for victory.

Ivar's sword crashed down, time after time, like a lightning bolt. Haakon threw up his shield and half crouched under it, while Ivar's sword split the shield nearly to the boss. The tip of Ivar's sword tore open Haakon's face from cheek to chin. At the same time the golden ax rose and swung sideways. The ax bit deeply into Ivar's leg below his armor. He howled and danced backwards on one foot. A second sword cut, which would have cracked Haakon's skull, struck only gravel as Haakon desperately rolled aside. As he came up onto his knees the golden ax drove into Ivar's leg again, just below the first cut. Ivar crumbled to his knees as Haakon rose to his feet.

Men watching the fight saw Haakon hesitate. Knowing the hatred he harbored for Ivar, Haakon refused to strike until he was sure that his own thoughts and the strength of his own arms guided the golden ax, not some power from a world beyond. Then the golden ax brushed Ivar's shield aside as if it were a piece of parchment and bit halfway into Ivar's neck. His death was bloody but mercifully quick. Haakon loomed large over Ivar's motionless body. Erik moved to Haakon's side, then motioned to two of Ivar's men to remove the corpse.

Haakon lowered the ax with one hand, wiped the blood from his face with the back of the other, and turned to Ivar's men. "Your chief is gone," he said, hoarsely. He couldn't have spoken louder if Odin himself asked it. "Your chief is gone, but my promise to all of you is still good. I wish nothing but peace now, and none of you will lose honor or weregild by swearing it."

Gunnar's voice came from behind him, apparently advising Ivar's men in poetry, but Haakon couldn't be sure of the words. His blood pounded in his temples and bile gurgled in his throat. He saw Ivar's men lowering their weapons and looking at each other. Then he raised his voice. "Choose six men to speak for you. We'll meet tonight in Ivar's hall to talk more of this peace. For now, Ivar's steading is mine!"

Some of Ivar's men raised their weapons again at these words. Others closed around them, disarmed them, and herded them aside until there was a clear path downhill for Haakon. Now Erik took Haakon's shield and steadied his stance while Rosamund was wiping the blood from his face with a wet cloth. He was grateful to them both. Gunnar came up to the Dane, gripped his forearm, and pronounced loudly:

> *Wave Walker*'s men followed Haakon
> To honor, dignity, and wealth.
> The men of Ivar Egbertsson may take
> this path of peace
> Or choose a life of strife, turmoil, and war.
> Which road would   wise man walk?

XIX

By the time Haakon entered what had been Ivar's chamber, Rosamund was asleep in the bed with Wulf's head on her shoulder. He could see nothing of her except her freshly washed hair trailing across the furs and the pale tip of one ear. She looked peaceful enough, in spite of their shared grief and doubts about their child.

It would be a while before those doubts were ended, one way or another. Certainly Rosamund had been through enough to make ten women miscarry. On the other hand,

Rosamund was a young and healthy woman. As yet, she had experienced no ominous flowing of blood.

Haakon realized that he was not yet ready for sleep, in spite of his wounds, bruises, and exhaustion. Such a day as this he'd never lived through before, and he rather hoped it would be a while before he lived through another such. He turned as Wulf whined softly and stayed with Rosamund. Haakon closed the door silently behind him, and strode outside.

It was a cool night with fog over the Trondelag and along the shore. Haakon walked a few paces, then sat down with his back to a solid pile of firewood. He no longer feared Ivar's men, but he still hadn't made definite arrangements for managing Ivar's steading. He'd have to do that quickly and leave a good band of men to protect his new property.

After dinner, Erik the Bald had once again broached the subject of marriage to Sigrid now that the battle with Ivar was ended and the uncle was aware of his nephew's true nature. Erik again swore an oath to return Sigrid's lands to Haakon if she should die before her husband, but no one considered it to be necessary now that Ivar was dead. Erik had insisted, however, and no one objected out of deference to him.

The Trondelag was suspicious of men too greedy for wealth and land. If Haakon simply ruled Ivar's steading as his own, he might find himself facing new enemies. He had hoped that Sigrid and Erik would be willing to assume responsibility for Ivar's land, but that would not be possible, due to how much land Sigrid and Erik already owned. Haakon considered Bosa, once he was freed, or possibly Gunnar and Guthrun after they were married. There were certainly enough people Haakon could trust with this steading.

Managing the land was the biggest piece of work to be done. Otherwise, Haakon could hope that today's victory was complete. Most of Ivar's men had sworn allegiance to him. They might not follow him on raids to Ireland, but they would not stab him or his people in the back at home either. A few would not swear at all, and he'd promised them all the money Ivar owed them and the freedom to go where they would.

Haakon suspected that there would not be much left of Rosamund's kidnapping price by the time he'd paid his mon and also distributed the promised wergild. He was not worried. Ivar had good fields and pastures. His herds were fat and his storehouses full. His steading was a prize richer than much silver, and meanwhile Haakon would have fewer discontented men near him.

There was also *Dragon Queen*. Through the fog Haakon saw the glow of torches and heard voices. Snorri and his men were surveying the work needed to repair the longship. "Ten days and she'll float again," he'd said. When Haakon sailed to Ireland next year, he would have three longships. He would need more spearmen to man all three properly, but he would need them anyway, if what he heard about Olaf Haraldsson's strength—

Ireland? The voice in his mind was definitely asking a question. Haakon stood up and raised the golden ax.

"Ireland," he announced in a voice that allowed no argument. Then he listened both to his thoughts and to the darkness around him for another question. None came. He rested the ax on his shoulder and started back toward the house and Rosamund.

Perhaps the question came from the gods, and perhaps his answer would not please them. Haakon did not care. He was grateful to the lords of Valhalla. They had given him the golden ax, the finest weapon he'd ever imagined. They'd guided him to Rosamund, and since he was not Gunnar, he had no real words for what she meant to him. He only knew that the thought of not having her beside him to warm him, strengthen him, bring him wisdom, and bear his children nearly made his heart stop with grief. He also knew that he would always feel this way, in all the years they might have together.

Yet two gifts were still not enough to buy him. Though the gods might in time have more work for him, now he had work of his own. His father would be avenged, and if the gods could not endure having as their servant a free man of the Norse, let them look elsewhere and see what they found.

It began to rain as he entered the house. He fell asleep beside Rosamund and Wulf with the sound of rain drumming on the roof.

Glossary

curragh: small boat made of wickerwood and covered with hide.

forswear: to renounce an oath or to swear falsely.

Hel: in Scandinavian mythology, the underworld region where spirits of men who died in their beds reside, as distinguished from Valhalla, the abode of heroes slain in battle.

jarl: tribal chieftain.

knarr: broad-beamed ship, deep in the water, with a high freeboard.

Norns: deities who tended men's destinies.

skald: Norse reciter or singer of heroic epics, a poet.

spaewife: female fortune-teller or witch.

thane: retainer or free servant of a lord.

Thing: northern assembly of free men for law, debate, and matters of regional importance.

thrall: a member of the lowest social class; a slave to a master or lord as a result of capture or an accident of birth.

wadmal: coarse, woolen material used for protective covering and warm clothing.

weregild: a value set by law upon the life of a man, in accordance with a fixed scale. Paid as compensation to kindred or to the lord of a slain person.

wyrd: fate.

COMING IN FALL 1984 ...
HAAKON: BOOK 3
HAAKON'S IRON HAND
by Eric Neilson

Haakon is plagued by peril when he defies the god Thor to
settle a blood-feud. Battling against fierce weather and the
machinations of a greedy king, Haakon is caught in a vicious
war between two savage peoples before he can attempt to
exact ultimate revenge against his archenemy Harud Olafsson.

Read HAAKON'S IRON HAND, on sale in the early fall,
1984, wherever Bantam paperbacks are sold.

Haakon-3

SPECIAL
MONEY SAVING
OFFER

Now you can have an up-to-date listing of Bantam's hundreds of titles plus take advantage of our unique and exciting bonus book offer. A special offer which gives you the opportunity to purchase a Bantam book for only 50¢. Here's how!

By ordering any five books at the regular price per order, you can also choose any other single book listed (up to a $4.95 value) for just 50¢. Some restrictions do apply, but for further details why not send for Bantam's listing of titles today!

Just send us your name and address plus 50¢ to defray the postage and handling costs.